Luna Station Quarterly

Issue 027 | September 2016

Editor & Publisher

Jennifer Lyn Parsons

Assistant Editors

Tara Calaby
Cathrin Hagey
Andi Marquette
Dana Mele
Megan Patton
Danielle Perry
Iona Sharma

Cover Artist

Sara Kipin

LUNA STATION PRESS

Luna Station Quarterly publishes short fiction on March 1st, June 1st,
September 1st, and December 1st. For more information and submission
guidelines, please visit our website at lunastationquarterly.com

For Luna Station Press

Creative Director - Tara Quinn Lindsey

LUNA STATION PRESS

576 Valley Road #197

Wayne, NJ 07470

www.lunastationpress.com

info@lunastationpress.com

CONTENTS

EDITORIAL

Jennifer Lyn Parsons

The world is a strange, dark and dangerous place. There are definitely times and places and venues where exploring that darkness, understanding it, making art while wielding its power is important and useful. But more often than not, I find uplift to be even more useful in beating back that same darkness and keeping hope alive that things can get better both in my own life and in the larger world.

I have no delusions that everything can and always should be happy-go-lucky. We all face trials that make us stronger when we take them on without shying from the challenges they bring. However, I do believe in the power of story to keep us afloat when times get hard. Stories can bring new perspective and a more positive outlook on life. It is said that books, movies, etc. are escapism. I say yes, they are, but that is not the a bad thing in the least when done with intention.

I'll quote Neil Gaiman here, for he summed up my feelings quite accurately here:

> *Fairy tales are more than true: not because they*
> *tell us that dragons exist, but because they tell*
> *us that dragons can be beaten.*

Dragons, trolls, evil stepmothers, they all represent obstacles in our own lives that we face and must overcome. Story gives us a map, provides a pattern that we may follow, an example of how to look these monsters dead in the eye and fight for our own happiness.

There is nothing wrong with a story that has dark tones to it, but that does not always have to be the centerpiece of the tale, nor does it have to go to extremes. Not all stories must contain violent, horrific imagery that leaves a reader almost as devastated as the character that had to live through that experience.

Everyone has a right to read and write those tales if they feel drawn to them and I do believe they are important both for the writer and the reader. But I choose not to make Luna Station Quarterly a venue for those pieces. LSQ is built upon a foundation of uplift, of showing what women are capable of writing, of the stories only they can tell. It is not a goal of ours to show how women are better than men, but in true diversity, to show that we are equal yet still unique.

Representation is exceedingly important, that's being proven daily as people step forward and question why they are not able to see themselves and their experiences mirrored in the stories they see on page and screen. As an editor, it's a difficult balance to maintain so that LSQ represents and provides a space for lesser heard voices and experiences, which often have much darkness in them due to the very systems and environments that suppressed their voices in the first place, while still maintaining that overarching theme of uplift.

Uplift is part of why we have a policy against accepting stories that contain a large amount of violence in them and generally do not accept stories that contain explicit sexual assault. Oddly enough, I don't think we've ever rejected a story for having too much bad language or positive sexual acts even though both would fall under the category of "gratuitous". I would personally love to have to ask an author to tone down the f-bombs or a fun love scene.

Does there need to be peril, danger, excitement, intrigue and challenge to make a good story? Of course there does, those are what pull a reader in and keep them intrigued. And this mission of uplift is not as simple as "we don't take rape stories" because the editors weigh each story for it's importance and impact as well as its grammar and characterization. Sometimes a hint of a character's violent past is necessary and we weigh that against the rest of the tale.

For now though, LSQ remains a magazine a bastion for stories of uplift. Sometime a thread of melancholy winds it's way through our tales, sometimes death and darkness touches the characters within, but always there remains a focus on wonder and beauty and hope for a better world for all of us.å

LSQ|027

THE DRAGON'S DINNER

Lindsey Duncan

Lindsey Duncan is a chef / pastry chef, professional Celtic harp performer and life-long writer, with short fiction and poetry in numerous speculative fiction publications. Her contemporary fantasy novel, Flow, is available from Double Dragon Publishing, and her soft science fiction novel, Scylla and Charybdis, is pending from Kristell Ink. She feels that music and language are inextricably linked. She lives in Cincinnati, Ohio.

Risantha grimaced as something squelched under her palm, releasing an odor worse than the priests who claimed shaving was against their religion. When her father and maker had told her princesses didn't get their hands dirty, she had blithely told him she would do what she had to do. She hadn't realized how literal "dirty" would be.

She crawled through the cramped cave tunnel, hoping the back way she had found would pay off. She would have to wriggle feet-first to retreat.

A flicker of light caught her attention. She huffed out a relieved breath, but remained tense. The dragon had defeated several seasoned knights who were, if not the best swords of the land, then passingly good...the sort of men who would strive for the hand of a princess who was blotch-skinned and had eyes the color of hardened leather. She hadn't mourned for any until the last: Kaulin, a sweet young man whose family had been llama herders until his father was knighted.

For Kaulin, then. She hoped her lessons in sword-dancing from her vociferously unmarried aunt would be enough. She fully intended to catch the dragon by surprise: this chivalry nonsense was an excellent way to become an h'ors doeuvre.

The light expanded into a glow, illuminating a ceiling pockmarked with stalactites. Her secret way seemed to come out at the top of the massive cavern. Clouds of smoke wafted towards her. Instinctively, Risantha held her breath…but not soon enough to prevent a wash of heavenly aroma from swimming through her nose.

Saffron and cloves, along with the tang of wood smoke. It smelled better than her adoptive mother's birthday feast – where, of course, the matriarch's age had been a state secret. The golems had carried in a cake without a single candle.

Risantha wriggled until she could see the cavern floor. The sight was so astonishing the last thing she noticed was the dragon.

Young men dressed in white rushed about, moving between cookpots the height of a person and tables piled with every conceivable fruit and vegetable, and some she couldn't conceive of that were bright blue or checkered. The clang of metal echoed like a joust, but the sound came from the contact of cooking implements.

The dragon supervised with a satisfied, matronly air, her head tilted just so and her eyes narrowed to inspection squint. Gold and pearl coils extended thrice as long as a royal wedding train – which was, to be precise, ridiculously long.

Risantha suppressed a gasp as she saw the bobble of Kaulin's nut-brown curls. Her heart bounced in her throat, disrupting the delicate mechanisms of her body. He was all right! Was he being held captive here? What about the others? She frowned, dredging up memories. These were the other knights who had ridden out to slay the dragon.

Could the dragon be holding them all? If they rushed her as one, surely she could not stop them…and the frenetic faces below seemed eager, not frightened.

Risantha peered down at a sequence of rocks that might serve for handholds. If she could climb quietly, perhaps she could get answers…or at the very least, sneak a taste. She had the tongue of a noted epicure, after all.

She felt exposed as she worked her way down. Thankfully, the chivalrous chefs never looked up, and the dragon paid attention only to their work.

"Start more stock." The walls reverberated with the order. Risantha squeaked, her foot slipping. She clung to the rock, almost breaking a stitch in her arm with the strength of her grip. She managed to brace her knee against the wall before the thump of her body could draw attention.

She risked a look below. The kitchen knights scrambled to obey the order. In the renewed chaos, she finished her descent, dropping to the ground. She found herself not far from a laundry basket with piles of soiled white outfits; she shrugged one on.

Head ducked, she darted through the culinary confusion until she reached Kaulin's cookpot. His head tilted up as she approached, and his eyes widened – surprise first, then a flash of delight followed by alarm. He hooked her arm with a ladle.

"Risantha?" he whispered. "What are you doing here?"

"Rescuing you," she said.

He blinked. "I don't need to be rescued. I'm staying because I like it here." His face flushed, an apologetic quiver coming to his lips. "I love you, Ris, but I'd never win you without defeating the dragon, and if I even tried…the other knights would swarm me."

She risked a glance at the immense, scaly supervisor, thinking. This was not just a wrinkle she had not expected, it was a ruined wardrobe. She knew better than to try and charm her erstwhile suitors. It was true, she had unique talents that would serve her in a fight, but she would just as soon not be cut down to size only to lose and…what? Go into a soup pot?

It was only then she realized what he had said. Her initial urge was to swoon, much as her constitution was not that of a typical lady. She lifted widened eyes to his face. "I love you, too," she said, "but you can't stay here. The dragon has been terrorizing -"

"You, with the dirty uniform!" The dragon's voice flooded the cavern, drawing every eye to her. "Have you no pride in yourself?"

Kaulin paled, instinctively moving to shield her with his body. The other knights turned, staring. She ducked her head hastily to hide her face, hand going to her sword...then sliding away. He was right: she couldn't defeat the dragon and all the knights.

The dragon huffed impatiently. "Speak up!"

"It was my fault," Kaulin said. "I splashed he... err, him."

"Look at me," the dragon commanded, "or I will scoop you out of the kitchen myself."

Trapped, Risantha tilted her chin up in what she hoped was a defiant fashion. "You will not get away with this," she said.

The low rumbling that vibrated the floor sent a chill of terror up her spine...until she realized it was laughter. She blinked, vaguely indignant. She knew she wasn't a particularly credible threat, but the dragon could at least contain her amusement.

"Get away," the creature finally said, "with what?"

"Terrorizing the peasantry," Risantha said, righteously sure of that much. "Stealing cattle and grain carts."

"Err, Risantha..." Kaulin murmured.

"I've never terrorized anyone. Royal propaganda." The dragon snorted. "And do you know what I do with the ingredients I requisition?"

Risantha hesitated. There didn't seem to be a polite way to point out how obvious it was.

"I feed your poor, your luckless, your prone-to-burning-their-houses-down - which is a larger percentage than you might think – with the finest haute cuisine." One pearly shoulder undulated. "I'm doing your kingdom a favor."

"It's true," Kaulin said. "I've helped distribute the meals."

Risantha pursed her lips, trying to look wise as the world spun around her. Everything she believed had been turned on its ear. Could she take the dragon at her word? The proof surrounded her...and Kaulin spoke it without fear or hesitation. That was enough.

"Then I need to go back to my father," she said, "and tell him what's really going on. He'll stop hunting you...if I bring someone with me who can describe your efforts." She looked significantly at Kaulin.

"Not so fast," the dragon said. "We're making princess soup."

Kaulin inhaled. "You can't be serious!"

Risantha remained calm; her heart never skipped a beat. "How much meat do you require?"

The creature peered down, scaly brows furrowing. "About a pound, I should think, but ..."

Risantha pulled aside the neckline of her tunic and found the subtle seam in the flesh of her shoulder. She popped the chunk of flesh free. The nearest knights gaped.

"Will this do?" she said.

"Very nicely," the dragon said. "I didn't realize you were a flesh golem, princess. Take your messenger and your message with you, with my blessing."

Kaulin continued to stare. "But...how...?"

Risantha flashed him a smile. "When my father offered my hand to the person who could defeat the dragon," she said, "what did you think he meant?"

REST STOP

MJ Gardner

MJ Gardner is a web developer by day, who lays in bed at night and wonders, what if....? The result is fantasy, horror and science fiction stories that are mostly (but not all) dark.

Her first book, Evelyns' Journal, is available on Amazon, Smashwords and other etailers.

It was on the long drive from Michigan to Denver, where her youngest daughter lived, that Marcy stopped at the gas station. It looked like it had been abandoned in the middle of a renovation. The ground all around it was dug up, and weeds as tall as her hips sprouted here and there between clods of dirt. She had to pee badly enough that she wasn't going to be picky.

She was taking the back roads rather than the interstate because when Lenny got home from his long-haul assignment to San Diego and found both her and his pickup gone he just might report the truck stolen.

The parking lot looked like a junkyard. Somebody had ideas about repairing old cars but never quite got around to it. Marcy's father's house had been like that. The junkers sitting in the weeds and in the woodlot became homes to squirrels and feral cats and once, to skunks. The skunks had been the final straw. Her mother insisted he get rid of the cars; it had been easier to move.

It was a lesson Marcy had put to good use. If you had a problem you couldn't fix, you moved on and left it behind. Like Lenny. Lenny was a big, fat, cheating, lying bastard

A sign that said 'Washrooms' pointed toward the back of the building. Marcy armed herself with one of the paper toilet seat covers she had picked up at the TA Travel Center and a wad of tissue.

The grey-aged plywood door had a cheap handle, like you would put on a cupboard. Marcy hoped there was a slide bolt on the inside, but then, there didn't seem to be anyone around to worry about.

The door made a predictable squeal and banged shut behind her on rusty spring-loaded hinges. Marcy pushed her sunglasses up onto the top of her head. In front of her an unpainted cinder block wall blinked into focus as her eyes adjusted to the gloom. She turned to the left and there was nothing, just a blank plywood wall, no sink, and to the right... there was another plywood wall and no toilet. Like the outside of the gas station, the bathroom wasn't finished. Marcy gave a snort—half exasperation and half laughter— and turned. She wasn't too proud to pee in the weeds out back. She put her hand against the door and pushed.

It wouldn't move.

There was no handle on this side, no latch and no slide bolt. Marcy frowned at the door and pushed again, then pushed with the flats of both hands. The door, which had felt flimsy when she opened it, was rock solid now. A dazzling strip of daylight outlined it, overpowering the feeble bulb over-head, but when she pounded on it, the door didn't so much as rattle.

'Hey! Anybody out there?' She punctuated her calls with bangs on the door. 'Hello?'

Marcy patted her pockets but her phone was in the truck. Was she going to have to wait for the next passerby? How long would that be? She needed to pee.

And then the floor started to tremble. Marcy felt more than heard a motor running, vibrating up the bones of her legs. With a jerk the room that was not a washroom started to move down. She put a hand out to steady herself against the cinder block wall but it was moving upward and she fell back against the very steady plywood door. A little pee leaked out before she could stop it.

The cinder block wall rolled by, upward, like the credits of a movie. Then came hard-packed dirt layered with chunks of bone-white limestone, and more and more limestone, until it was a solid, irregular wall.

With a gentle thud the box came to rest and the rumbling stopped.

'What the hell?'

Cool air washed over Marcy's legs. There as an opening, about three feet high at the base of the limestone wall and she crouched down to peer into it. A cleft in the rock, big enough to walk through, twisted away from the washroom-cum-elevator into darkness; there was no promising glare of sunshine at the end of it.

Marcy turned and looked at the makeshift elevator. There must be controls somewhere. Who builds an elevator without light-up, numbered buttons? The only surface that was not a solid full sheet of plywood was in the corner of the floor. There was a foot-square patch, like something had been cut out of the main sheet. Marcy thumped and banged at it and around it, but she wasn't able to pop open any secret lock. Where was MacGyver when she needed him? She tried pulling up the square, but there wasn't enough of a gap for her fingers to get purchase, and when she tried to pry with her keys, all she managed to do was break off splinters. The square was more solid than the rest of the floor.

'Go back up!' cried Marcy, banging on the door again. 'Let me out!' There was no echo. 'My boyfriend is right behind me. He's gonna see my truck and want to know where I am,' she called. There was no response. 'He's got his dog and his huntin' rifles with him!'

Nothing.

Well wouldn't her sister Darlene be happy to see this? It would be proof to her that Marcy never should have left Lenny, and never headed out cross-country on her own. When she told Darlene she was leaving him, her sister had said that at sixty-two she was no spring chicken and she ought to overlook Lenny's little faults and hang on to him. Darlene was a prude who thought she deserved a merit badge for only ever having slept with the same man for the past 40 years. Marcy told her sister that it was better to be alone than to wish you were, although it was a theory that she had never actually tested out.

Every time Marcy left a man—or he left her—it seemed there was another one waiting in the wings. She wasn't the sort of woman who was supposed to attract men: she was short and plump and her dishwater blond curls had gone grey early on. But they liked her smile, and they called her sweet and cuddly and fun.

No one would ever call Darlene fun.

Marcy bent to look into the passage at her feet again. There was an uneven floor was about three feet below the opening, like the elevator had not quite made it to the bottom.

Did the passage lead out? Was it a disused but still function-ing funhouse rid? Were people in the safety and comfort of their homes watching her now via hidden cameras? Or was there a chainsaw-wielding psycho at the other end of that passage wearing someone else's skin and waiting to add Marcy's to his wardrobe?

And then she heard something coming down the passage.

Marcy crab-walked herself back into a corner. She wished she had a baseball bat, or better, a gun, and then she remembered all the women's self-defense advice she had read. She slipped Lenny's keys between her trembling fingers. Truck key, house key, shed key, shop key, other keys she didn't know. His ratty and faded green rabbit's foot dangled at her wrist. She crouched, braced against the plywood corner, so she had a good view into the passage.

A girl's pale face appeared around a bulge in the rock. Marcy relaxed a little, but she didn't let go of the keys. The girl paused and looked Marcy over, then proceeded to pick her way carefully along the corridor towards the elevator.

Marcy felt less relieved when she got a close-up look at the girl. Dark hair hung in greasy strands around her face, like yarn, and she squinted at the weak light. Blue veins pulsed beneath translucent skin. A too-large dress hung from shoulders so thin they could have been made out of a wire coat hanger.

'Are you going to come out?' asked the girl in a papery, inflectionless voice.

'What's out there?' asked Marcy.

The girl looked behind her, as if checking to see if the landscape had changed, and then looked back at Marcy. 'The pool,' she said.

A vision of the community pool in the trailer park where Marcy had lived after they moved from the junkyard house flashed on her mind's eye: glittering chlorinated water and sunshine and boys and the ice cream truck. But she didn't think this girl's pool was like that.

'Is there a way out?'

'Out?'

'Back to the gas station? To the parking lot?'

'It leads to the pool. That's all. That's all there is.'

'I want to go back up.'

The girl shook her head. 'It won't go up when anyone is in it.'

Marcy stared at her. 'How did you get down here?'

'The same way you did.'

'How long have you been down here?'

The girl shrugged, twined her hands together in front of her hips, so that her elbows pointed out and started twisting gently side to side.

'There's no way out?' Marcy asked again.

'Mm mm.'

'You live down here?'

'Mm hm.'

'How do you live? What do you eat?'

'Fish. Mushrooms. Lichen, but not the glowing kind. We need that for light.'

Marcy looked at the pale and undernourished girl. 'People who come down in this elevator?' she suggested.

The girl stopped her twisting motion. 'There was a man once. He wouldn't come out. He starved to death. We took his body out. Then the elevator went back up.' The girl pointed and looked up as if she was referring to a mythical place.

'I want to go back up,' Marcy declared.

'Do you have anything?' asked the girl.

'Anything like what?'

'Matches. Or a lighter? Or gum? I had gum once. It was orange. It was so good. But that was a long time ago.'

'No. Just me and my truck keys.'

'Can I have them?'

Marcy shook her head. Apparently the girl had never read any self-defense advice to women and didn't know that the keys' Freddy Kruger arrangement between her fingers was meant to be a weapon.

'Are you going to come out?'

'I want to go back up,' Marcy repeated.

The girl shrugged and turned away and went back down the passage the way she had come.

Marcy lowered her bottom to the floor to sit. The crotch of her shorts was uncomfortably damp. Someone would come. Someone else would stop for the same reason she had and find a gaping elevator shaft. They might curse out loud or call their buddy over to look, and she would hear them, and she would call for help and they would get her out. Or Lenny would come looking for his truck. Or the police. Someone would rescue her.

Marcy rolled onto her side so she could see into the passage better. She was looking for the glinting eyes of little hidden cameras. If they could see her, surely she could find them. After all, this couldn't be real. But in the feeble light all she saw was rock and more rock.

Why couldn't Lenny be one of those handy types with a flashlight on his keychain instead of the blasted rabbit's foot? It hadn't done the rabbit any good, and it wasn't doing her any good either.

And then the light snapped off. Marcy caught a scream of surprise behind her hands. And she peed. Not all of it, but more than a trickle. She cursed under her breath. When someone did rescue her they were going to see that she had peed her pants like a little girl. Or an old lady.

Stress incontinence, the doctor called it. It's age, he had said, with his condescending smile. She wanted to tell him that one day age would get him too, and his prostate would explode.

This was the same doctor who had called her in for a checkup when she wasn't due for one, told her she had a yeast infection, which she knew she didn't have, and gave her a shot and a scrip for antibiotics. Her friend Hester at the pharmacy told her the antibiotics were for the clap. Lenny had given it to her. And where had Lenny picked it up? Not from her, that was damn sure.

'Alright, let's be calm and reasonable. There's nothing here in the dark that wasn't here in the light,' she said out loud. 'I have two problems: I am stuck down here, and I have to pee.'

Marcy climbed to her feet and dropped her shorts and her underwear. She didn't want to pee on the floor when it was the only place she had to sit. There was no dignified way to stick her behind out into the passage. On her knees she crawled backwards to the opening, rolled onto her back, braced her feet against the limestone like she was giving birth, and shot her pee out into the darkness of the passage.

That felt so much better. She hoped the undernourished cannibal girl stepped in it.

Dried off and dressed again, Marcy contemplated the passage. She didn't want to get out precisely because that was the only option she seemed to have. He or she or it wanted her to get off the elevator. And then the elevator would leave without her and she'd be stranded with the pale girl cannibal.

But then again staying put wasn't much of an option. She had a vision of herself starved to death in the elevator and the denizens of this underground chamber of horrors creeping along the passage to claim her body for dinner. The girl would pluck the truck keys from her limp fingers and smile smugly over her useless new treasure.

Or maybe they wouldn't wait for her to starve.

Marcy finger-combed her hair and reset the sunglasses on her head. She took a deep breath and straightened her shoulders. She was not going to let that happen.

The cannibal girl had said: it won't go up with anybody in it. So how did the elevator know if someone was in it? Marcy stood up and walked back and forth. Yes, there was some give to the floor. There had to be a pressure plate underneath. That's why there were no buttons: the floor was the button. Push it, you went down; release it, you went up.

She had to get off the floor. No matter where she stood, she was pressing down on that switch.

And then she remembered the square of firmly nailed-down plywood in the corner. It didn't lift to reveal controls: it was the exact opposite. The whole floor was a switch and it wasn't.

Marcy squeezed herself into the corner, scuffling for the edges of the plywood square with the toes of her sandals to make sure she was on it. She held the position, held her breath, and then the trembling of the motor started. With a cry of happy surprise she let the tension of her body go, she lost her balance, and one foot came down on the main part of the floor.

The motor stopped and the elevator thumped back down.

There was a faint noise. Someone was coming way down the passage.

'You can do it,' she told herself. 'You have to do it.'

Marcy crammed herself back into position, willing her round body to fit into the ninety-degree angle like a corner cupboard. Oh, to be twelve again, and skinny!

The person in the passage was not in a hurry, but they were getting closer.

Go! She silently urged the elevator.

And it did. It started to tremble and then, with a jerk, it moved upward. Marcy pressed the palms of her hands flat against the plywood walls to hold herself steady, splinters be damned. She stayed that way until the elevator not only stopped, but the trembling motor shut off.

And then she counted to three.

On three she sprang for the door. It bounced open with a squeal of rusty springs and Marcy tumbled out in to the twilight, scraping her forearms and knees first on the broken concrete of the sidewalk, and then on the gravel of the parking lot. She staggered to her feet, ran for the truck and wrenched open the door.

Marcy shot out of the lot spewing gravel behind her. She drove as fast as she dared until she reached a ramp for the interstate and a proper truck stop, lit up like a ballpark for a night game. She sat in the parking lot while she caught her breath, and pulled out a map.

No more back roads. She was hitting the interstate.

INTO THE STARFISH HEART

J.M. Wetherell

J.M. Wetherell lives and works
in New York City. She is a 2015
graduate of Clarion West.

What remains to be said about Ledo? Between the retrospectives upon retrospectives, the steady flow of monographs spooling from the critics these forty-odd years, not a leaf is left unturned in the artist's gardens. I am looking out on them this afternoon, in all their verdant blush, sipping iced tea in the bright light of sunlamps while my old acquaintance sketches the icy peaks of their personal mountain range beyond the great glass dome in the distance. Acquaintance is the term I will use, for though we first met years ago I feel I know Ledo no better or worse than those who have skimmed over their strange life's details in the tabloids.

In the end, only one entity in the cosmos will know the privilege of a greater intimacy with the artist, a greater understanding. The void that lies at the heart of our galaxy is waiting, silently, ready to welcome into invisible arms its first living citizen in several billion years. Ledo in their small craft, drifting steadily to oblivion, performing till the end - when they will be promptly rendered apart, in an automatic and indifferent act of murder.

Change the subject, of course, and it is a suicide. Although Ledo does not see it that way, some weeks before the performance is scheduled to occur, as we sit on the terrace high above the gardens, bathed in electric daylight and turning under the dome of eternal night. The artist's studio and residence is located in a climatologically isolated dome on the ice moon of Wreade, a construction that was supervised by Ledo's longtime patrons, the Fanfax siblings, Helena and Clem, heirs to their family's agricultural empire. Where we sit it is pleasantly, summerishly warm; the sloping green valley before us is filled with flowering trees and running brooks. Beyond that there is ten meters thick of glassy forcefield, and beyond that are black mountain peaks ravaged in permanent snowstorm, next to which this habitat has been dropped like an enormous fishtank.

"I was made to last five years. And today I am twenty-seven. Obscene!" Ledo puts down the pen and paper and knits together small gray-skinned hands, gleefully. "So it is fitting, something quite obscene."

With their boyish soft face and black knit cap, they are a compact and rounded-seeming, like a strange doll, smiling slightly in a way that nonetheless betrays a great well of mirth. Observers of Ledo have oftentimes remarked on the strangeness of a scarecrow that smiles, that has an expression at all.

I ask if it is the upcoming Starfish Heart performance that is the obscenity. Ledo shakes their head. "No, no. This." They flick their wrist, tightly buttoned in black sleeves, out onto the landscape. "All this. A present for me."

Their tone turns half-mournful, half-mocking. Their eyes are still laughing, always laughing - at what, only Ledo can know.

**

Twenty-seven years ago, on a sunbaked day - the way of all days on Yadley VI, the sixth planet from the binary star in the Fanfax system - a child was born, in the fallow season. That is, one hundred children were born together, in the industrial compound at Y6-D in the southwest hemisphere. Thousands in total were born that day, across the seven compounds jointed together by checkerboarded field roads, running the planet's thick crops like scars on a green apple. While the Fanfax Corporation neglects to release the official numbers for the other side of its yearly harvest, the annual cloning and hatching of its agricultural workforce, estimations by our leading economists for the year of Ledo's birth saw a twofold jump from the previous ten, the beginning of a long upward tick in scarecrow production.

It was the hundred scarecrows in Ledo's cohort, companions and colaborers from birth in the fields of Yadley VI, that famously offered a subject for much of the artist's early work. Perhaps the most overt example is the well-known sculpture *Untitled (One Hundred Faces)*, which appeared in Ledo's second gallery show. While art students may note this was largely an exhibition of painting - the artist's first, some say finest, medium - it was the quite literally splashy centerpiece that charmed the cognoscenti and casual viewers alike. A whole room in the gallery was devoted to the piece, its walls blank apart from one hundred faucets running the perimeter in a perfectly straight line. Every few days Ledo would come in after-hours and turn on a new stream of water, leaving them to run day and night. Gallery-goers were obliged to don first rubber booties, finally wetsuits and airtanks as the installation progressed. Antifluid fields at the doorways protected artworks in adjacent galleries. It was simple; it was elemental. Children laughed and splashed about. Other patrons wept for the scarecrows, or said that the water was brined with tears, that they had tasted this as they swam.

I first encountered Ledo at this moment when the scales tipped, on the cusp of their arrival in the art world. They were more somber then, and still learning a faculty for language, so they spoke slowly. But they told me that day - a very young critic, and still quite somber myself - how the scarecrows were hydrated twice over the course of Yadley VI's thirty-five hour days, at first light and at sundown, with the long day of harvesting in between. I still have the tape from the recorder I was carrying, as we walked in the empty gallery, Ledo's halting voice as they described the contents of the solution they were given: "Eighty percent hydrous, six percent lipid, ten percent carbohydrate, trace amounts of various minerals, drugs." Fifteen years later, Ledo would serve the same concoction in cocktail shooters to crowds of eager patrons at the Quadrennialle. (It was pink, sweet, presented without explanation. Depending on their anatomies those who sampled remember a brief surge of elation, or a venomous distrust of those around them, or a simple yearning to lie limp on the floor, which this critic will attest to.)

Today, at the studio on Wreade, we walk down from the terrace into Ledo's gardens, and as their fingers linger on the purple blossoms lining the path they hum a tune, something atonal but distinctly repetitive. They have told me they did not hear music until they were taken from Yadley VI, that they are still getting the hang of it. Genetic engineering for contemporary Fanfax scarecrow models has phased out the phenotypical presentation of the oral cavity, teeth and vocal chords. When Ledo was born the scarecrow's mouths were still sealed shut shortly after birth with a biochemical adhesive, a false skin that sealed over the lips. Sustenance, then as now, is mediated entirely through a port each scarecrow unit bears in the abdomen. Today there are scarcely visible scars on Ledo's boyish face, from the corrective surgery that created their mouth. But the abdominal port they have never removed. At certain angles it is revealed as strange ripple under the thin fabric of the tunics they favor.

***

"How many years can you spend looking for something truly exciting, truly genius? You can waste a lifetime." Helena Fanfax glances out the window, into radiant starfield, and takes another drag of her cigar. "My father had established certain standards with his collection that my brother and I were given the duty to maintain. And yet the work that was being produced, before Ledo, was, by and large, pure shit."

We are on the stardeck of a low-orbit cruiser gently circling pink-and-blue-clouded Mylanthe, where the Fanfax estate occupies much of the central continent. In the last century the family's engineers have terraformed it into a huge island, circled by endless bathtub-warm seas. The moon Wreade, and Ledo's studio, bob somewhere in the distance. I have been pedaled over for the afternoon by a Fanfax transport to conduct the interview.

"It was all the same," mourns Clem Fanfax, walking over in his long peignoir; he says he is recovering from a full skin transplant. The age of the Fanfax siblings is not a matter of public record. He plucks another highball from the arm of a mechanized attendant. "System after system, the parade of dealers peddling these so-called 'folk-artists'—souvenir makers, I'd say..."

"Embarrassing," Helena scoffs. "Self-aware, hollow, meaningless—if there is not a spontaneous honesty at the beginning of the career, the genuine impulse to truth, then there really is nothing at all. And yet that was the nature of the work we saw for years, in every city, on every rotten little moon. In the schools it was the worst. There they'd studied our father's acquisitions, fetishized them. Endlessly predictable, year after year. For decades, nothing but astral projection, nanoconstruction..."

"Thought control," Clem chimes in.

"Knickknacks and trickery."

"Derivative. Awful."

"Can you understand, then, what it was, the moment we learned of this performance?" Helena rises, turning to stand before the glass, as Clem sits, eyes trailing his sister over the rim of his drink. "To see this impulse, this performance, from a mind that had no sense of art—could never have possibly— and therefore no sense of *dec*eption."

"In our own backyard, so to speak," Clem drawls, and drinks.

"We were bound to Ledo," Helena says. "My father loved artists all his life. And he helped them, all his life, those that he saw possessed the true spirit. The scarecrow was the way he made his fortune. To have genius arise spontaneously from that lifelessness—this is the greatest seed of his legacy, bearing fruit in the unlikeliest manner." She turns around, smiling. "Ledo was to be exterminated, you know, before we learned about their talent. We saved them. We *nam*ed them."

I ask where the name came from. Clem leans back and looks at his sister. "What was it? A dog? A fish? A dolphin?" He laughs. "Only some nonsense, a name for a pet. From when we were children."

Previously it would have been difficult to imagine the Fanfaxes as children; the joyous ripple in Helena's voice proves me wrong, suddenly, as she responds–the sound of a child opening a gift.

"Of course! I must have forgotten." For the first time she hints at a smile. She sighs. "That was where the name came from, a very innocent time in our lives. There was such innocence in that first performance."

The original video is still on display on a loop at Ledo's studio. It is stitched together from several security feeds at different angels, the same form it took in Ledo's first showing on the contemporary wing of the Galactic Institute. On Wreade I watch it several times, although Ledo never joins me.

In the video, it is night on Yadley IV, and a scarecrow walks, naked as all scarecrows, through the door of a squat concrete building. The feed then cuts to the interior, where a number of small bodies—the shot informs us of seven—are laid out on metal tables, unmoving. It is not clear whether they are living or dead. The standing scarecrow turns away, for a moment, to a desk at the front of the room, where a kit of surgical tools is spread open. When the scarecrow turns back around its mouth is wide open, bleeding. It holds a scalpel in its small gray hand. It shouts, silently on the feed, smiling. Black-looking blood is dripping out of its mouth, and it takes its hands to it, wiping them first to make dark marks on its body, then walking among the bodies on the tables, painting them with its fingers. Eyes on their foreheads, mouths on their chests. Thumbprints up and down their limbs. It fades to black as the scarecrow circles and circles the parts of the room we cannot see, before the guards come in, before its body is pinned to the floor.

Ledo has little to say on the subject of their early career. They claim to remember it poorly, that this is a defunct of the scarecrow brain. They often point to the cheapness and shabbiness of their body, taxed far beyond its years of optimal utility. They say they feel ancient, at twenty-seven.

I ask what they know about the fate of their fellow scarecrows, those born in the same year on Yadley VI. Ledo is certain that they we all repossessed in the months after the Fanfax family took interest in the video. This is the natural fate for scarecrows at the end of their time, for their matter to be broken down and sown back into the soil that was their world.

I ask Ledo about starfish, and they say they remember a tidal pool, some portion of the massive shoreline on Mylanthe, where thousands lived. They were standing in the water looking at the colony when a young Fanfax cousin came splashing down to pick up handfuls of the creatures. As Ledo stood watching she tore their limbs off and threw them back into the water, over and over.

"I asked the child why," Ledo says, leading me gradually to

the studio, over the stone path throw a shallow pond that connects it to the living quarters. "I suppose she was an amateur biologist, as she told me it was quite all right, that the arms grow right back. That it really wasn't a trouble to them at all."

***

The work, in its current form, is a small room inside of a small space-ship. The room is furnished with a simple bed, a table, a chair. There are no windows. There is a door that, once closed, will not open again. The walls are white. Ledo invites me to sit on the bed, and it is firm, with tight-creased white sheets. They sit before me in the white chair opposite the bed, and tell me about a second room being built inside of a second ship.

"A living room," Ledo says with a little laugh. "For the observers." The observation chamber is being constructed at the Fanfax residence on Mylanthe, by a crew under Ledo's supervision, along with the vessel that will contain it. The two ships—Ledo's, and the second, being built for the Fanfaxes and invited friends from the art circuit (it is a most coveted invitation), are said to be identical save for one detail. One is engineered to withstand the gravitational warp of the singularity in space, at the safe distance at which it will be positioned. The other has no such special qualities, and will in fact be aiming for the heart of it.

"The traveler may perish." Ledo smiles again. "And yet the journey will be infinite. At the threshold, I believe, there is a kind of time that slips inside of time, boxes in boxes in boxes, like this."

We go out into the bright glow of the lamps that light Ledo's home. There is a wilder garden here, tall grasses and vines that twist into thick boughs. Throughout their travels in the galaxy Ledo has collected plants, cultivating those they can in the dark soil that was found under Wreade's ice and snow. When it is all over, Ledo tells me, once the performance has occurred and the studio is left without its artist, the garden will overtake the grounds, spread though the buildings, grow unfettered under the dome and create what ecosystem it will. A clause covers this for a millennium in Ledo's contract with the Fanfax siblings, who are delighted by the prospect of yet another aspect to the commission – a living memorial, from organic chaos evolving a mind of its own.

**

Today I have been invited to bear witness to the Starfish Heart performance, as to provide a suitable conclusion to my article. I write these words in my eyepiece from the backseat of a Fanfax transport, which came floating down before my condo this sunrise. It has sped through the dark of space for several hours when it finally slows, going past a small flotilla of newsvans that have parked on the far periphery of the performance area. My transport is given the silent clearance to go on, closer to the event horizon.

My transport docks, and I am received through the threshold of the spectator ship, where a silent attendant leads me into the observation chamber. I am handed a glass of cordial, for toasting, and a pair of coated observation lenses, for the glare, both engraved with the entwined initials of Clem and Helena Fanfax.

The Fanfax decorators have had their hands on the interiors, which are reminiscent of the finer and more debaucherous hotel lounges—fat satin couches, an internal—organ color scheme, long, mirrored tables crowded with drinks and elbows. Laughter and conspiratorial murmurs fill the air, chatter and anticipation—of what, though? Very few of the invited spectators, for now, are viewing the spectacle on hand.

For we are drifting slowly forward, as I write these words,

into streaming starfield innocuous but for a radiant, pulsing blemish blinking in the distance, smaller than a sun, larger than a distant star and growing in size, slightly, by the second. Its colors queasy, glaring green and gold, shifting constantly, difficult to look at even with the special lenses - beautiful, all the same.

Beside the great observation window are dual screens, each displaying Ledo's room, in Ledo's ship. In the feed Ledo sits, motionless, unclothed, on the bed, the lumpy gray scar growth of their scarecrow port fully bared. Their face is in profile, licks of thin, sparse black hair covered normally by the cap sticking flying off of their gray forehead. Then the camera angle changes, head-on. Ledo blinks, twice. Ledo smiles.

The ship is gliding forward, more swiftly now it seems, as I turn back towards the party, feet sinking into the padded velvet carpet. I see Clem laughing, and Helena beside him, drinking, their invited revelers circling and circling, glasses clinking. They will go on for hours, days if they can. Their minds will be slowed by drink, and then the world will seem to warp and break. And it will. People will make confessions on the altars of each other's breasts, as their organs degrade, as their cry and claw at their slurring hearts, as everything is drawn impossibly thin, as if through a needle's eye, into brightness ever-growing.

Tears cloud my eye-typing apparatus, as I send these final words. My regret is that my testament cannot come any later, that I will never truly capture the artwork as it happens, what is sure to be counted among the most magnificent performances of our time or any. Yet soon it will inhabit its own time, its own infinite dissolution. Such is the signature of our greatest artists.

And now on the screens Ledo is rising, and smiling still, as if they can see us, as if it is they who are watching. The light is rising, with that huge darkness at the center. The work will soon incorporate us, and we should be so honored, as Ledo stands to watch.

MAMA TULU

Jessica Guess

Jessica Guess is a Florida native
and daughter of Jamaican
immigrants. She enjoys writing
tales of mystery, suspense,
and dark fairy-tale and reads
anything with female villains.
Jessica currently resides
in Minnesota where she is
an MFA candidate in the
Creative Writing program at
the Minnesota State University,
Mankato.

The road to Mama Tulu's shack was nearly impossible to trudge. There were no streetlights, no cleared trail, just rocks and dirt and bushes that reached halfway up my waist and scratched my calves. Makka bush, my mother called them, but I pushed her out of my mind. She'd curse me from morning to night if she knew where I was going. I tried to think about Robbie instead: his tall, lean frame, his long black dread locks, this army green jacket with the Lion of Judah printed on the shoulder like a stripe of honor. Since moving back to Jamaica, thinking of him was the only thing that could make me happy until, of course, thoughts of my father inevitably pushed them out. But hopefully that would end soon. Mama Tulu would end it.

The red dirt road left stains on the hem of my dress, but I didn't pay it any mind. I'd hide it until my mother went to sell goods at the market then wash it while she wasn't there. All around me I could hear the chirps of crickets, the hooting of owls, and all the other noises of the island's night creatures, but I couldn't see any of them. Only a bit further. Only a little bit. As if the Lord (or maybe something else) heard my plea, a light appeared a few yards ahead of me. I climbed the rest of the way up the bushy hill until finally, Mama Tulu's house was in front of me. It wasn't at all what I expected. Instead of the zinc roof hut I had pictured, there was a small house made of wood with vines of all types of bushes entwined around it. The front porch had vines and weeds all over the floor, nearly blocking the wood from view. I stood in awe of the place for a moment before the hairs on the back of my neck prickled. I looked around but saw nothing. The only visible thing was the house and the light coming from the inside of it.

I walked up the four steps onto the porch, the vines and leaves crunching underneath my feet. I raised my fist to knock but stopped short. What if she was asleep? What if I angered her by waking her up? Most of all, what was I doing here? Did I really want this? Before I could think of a real answer a voice startled me out of my thoughts.

"Ah what kind ah gyal just lingah in front of an ol' woman doorway dis yah hours ah night? Mus be lookin' fi trouble."

My breath caught in my throat. I looked around again, but saw nothing. "M-May I come in, Mama Tulu?"

There was silence for a long moment. I started to think that I imagined the voice until she finally spoke again.

"Come in, child."

Inside of Mama Tulu's house was like nothing I'd ever seen before. She directed me to sit down in a straw chair while she put a kettle on. I sat and tried not to look as frightened as I felt, but my eyes wondered around the room. There were vines hanging from the ceiling along with colored jars on the ends of ropes with shadowy substances inside of them, but nothing in her house was as strange in appearance as Mama Tulu herself. First of all, no one could tell the woman's age. She looked to be in her 50's but her hair was as white as cotton and cascaded down her back in a long messy braid, the front of it frizzy in her face. Her hands were wrinkled, but she always had painted nails, something none of the women over 30 did in this part of the country. Her skin was dark brown like mine, but her eyes were hazel and some-times seemed to glow, even the daytime when she walked in the market. She always wore a silvery mesh shawl over her dark purple or green dress and sometimes walked with an umbrella perched over her head to block off the sun.

"Nevah seen a stush Obeah woman," Miss Jacklyne said one day when Mama Tulu passed her fruit stand. She had waited until the old woman was out of earshot and leaned over to my mother as she stacked her yam and potatoes.

"Quiet for she tun yuh inna one ah 'ar Nameless," my mother said, flinching as she lifted an unusually heavy yam with her injured hand.

Mama Tulu turned to me, two cups in her hand. I straightened in my chair, a habit that formed from years of elders inspecting my posture. She handed me a cup of tea and kept one for herself before sitting in the chair opposite me. I looked at the cup. I wasn't sure if I should drink or not. You weren't supposed to eat or drink from Obeah women, but it was rude to not eat or drink as a guest in someone's home. I took a sip and she did the same, her eyes still on me over the rim of her cup. Ginger and mint flooded my taste buds before I swallowed.

"Whah yuh name?" she asked.

"Sasha."

"Sasha. Sasha," she said as if rolling the word around in her mouth to see if she liked the taste. "Yuh Maddah have a stand eh?"

"Yes, ma'am."

"Yuh talk nice. Nuh like them chat bad picknie ah street. Yuh nuh from Jamaica?"

"My parents moved to Florida when I was a baby, but we came back two years ago."

"Heh," Mama Tulu scoffed. "Go ah foreign an' come back? Supm' bad muss happen."

I nodded not sure if she wanted to know and not sure if I should tell her if she did.

She looked me up and down. "How old yuh be?"

"Fifteen."

"Fifteen," she repeated. "Is a bwoy yuh lookin'? Dah red bwoy wheh hang roun' yuh Maddah stand? Di dread?"

"No, ma'am."

"Good. Dread man is a likkle hardah fi catch. Whah yuh want?"

I opened my mouth then closed it again. Even up until now I wasn't sure that I was really going to do this, and even if I wanted to do it, could she do it? I thought of my mother's hand, now nearly useless, and how she limped for a week during the summer when we came back here.

"I want you to kill my father."

Mama Tulu stared at me for what seemed like an hour, then smiled. "Now, why yuh want supm' like that, gyal?"

I was hoping she wouldn't ask me that. I was hoping she would just tell me she couldn't do it and send me on my way, or tell me she could and tell me her price, but of course it wasn't so.

"He's a monster," I said and I wasn't lying. He was the reason we had to come back to Jamaica after eleven years in the United States. He drank away all of the money he worked and took the money my mother made cleaning houses and gambled it away. After a few losses he couldn't pay back, the people he owed came looking for him. They tried to beat him up but he fought back, injuring one of the men and putting the other one in a coma. His punishment was deportation and my mother said we had to leave the only home I'd ever known to come back with him. But that wasn't why he needed to die. Two weeks ago he beat my mother worse than any of the times before. I came back from school to find her laying on the floor, unconscious, her eyes swollen, and her hand twisted at an odd angle. For days she laid on her bed, barely able to move, until finally she could stand on her own again. And the first thing she did when she could was make him breakfast.

"Hmm," Mama Tulu said after I finished. She sipped her tea, then tilted her head to the side, thinking. "He's yuh faddah. Yuh real faddah?"

"Yes."

"Yuh sure?

"Yes. We look just alike."

She thought again. "And yuh sure yuh wan' kill him?"

"I want him gone."

"Seems cruelty run inna yuh family," she said and stared me in the eye.

I ignored the sting of her words and stared back.

After a moment she laughed and held out her hand. "Gimme yuh palm gyal."

She took my hand in her own and took out a long knife seemingly from nowhere. The handle was carved from ivory and had black engravings on it. The blade itself was long and pointed, half of it smooth but sharp, and the half closer to the handle, serrated so that it looked like teeth. My first instinct was to pull back my hand, but I held it steady. She pressed the tip into the palm of my hand until a trickle of blood spilled out of my broken flesh. She bowed her head to my hand then looked up at me again.

"Yuh absolutely sure?"

I nodded.

She put her mouth over the wound she created in the center

of my palm and sucked. Her tongue was wet and hot against my flesh but my entire body went cold and I felt as if she was sucking more out of me than just my blood. She was sucking my hatred, my anger, my pain. Finally she raised her head and shivered. "It's done."

***

For three days my father didn't so much as cough. He was completely normal. He went to his job mining bauxite in the morning then drank until he passed out if we were lucky. If he somehow managed to stay conscious we were sure to hear his endless cursing or worse. The third day I came home from helping my mother at the market to find him on the porch, a bottle of white rum in his hand.

"Where yuh maddah?" he said.

"She's coming. She's packing up everything."

He unscrewed the bottle cap and took a drink. "Dah Rasta bwoy came here lookin' fi yuh. Yuh tink say yuh a big 'oman now eh?"

I ignored him and stepped to go into the house but he stood up and blocked me.

"Yuh ah listen to me, gyal? Yuh nah take up with no dutty rasta bwoy, yuh hear me?"

"Better a dutty rasta than a useless drunkard," I said looking him in his eyes. They were a deep brown that brightened when the sunlight caught them, the same as mine.

I knew what was coming but it didn't help the impact of his blow. He caught me across my face sending me to the floor, then sat back down, pleased with himself. He took another swig from his bottle. I tried to steady the ringing in my ears but it was useless. I touched my lip and saw blood. I got to my feet, not looking at him, and went inside barely able to contain my anger. That damned obeah woman was a fraud.

He should surely be dead by now, not drinking on the porch. Maybe tomorrow I would go see Mama Tulu again.

A loud crash woke me up. Disoriented, I looked at my clock and saw that it was 3:15 in the morning. For a moment I thought that I dreamt the noise before a louder crash echoed throughout the house. My mother screamed and I ran to her room, sure that I would find my father on top of her again, his fists raised in the air, but instead she was sitting above him shaking his shoulders.

"Errol? Errol?" she cried but he didn't answer.

His eyes were wide open and glazed over. His mouth was twisted to the side and slack. The cold feeling returned and ran though my body before leaving me there alone with my mother and father.

The doctor said that he'd had a stroke and that we had to try to feed him as best we could. The nearest hospital was miles away and we couldn't afford it even if it was closer. He wasn't dead but he couldn't talk or move. He just laid there, staring up at the ceiling. The doctor came to check on him every day and every day he said that his was getting worse, his pulse getting weaker. Finally, a week later, the doctor pronounced him dead, but when he tried to close his eyelids, my father's eyes refused to shut. They stuck stubbornly like a door blown open in a hurricane. My mother tried shut them, as well as her cousin and his brother, but nothing could make them close.

***

The funeral was closed casket because of the eyes. My mother cried and shook the entire service as I tried my best to hold her steady.

"Nuh worry yuhself," Miss Jacklyne whispered to my mother."Him in a better place."

"Him suffer that entire week. Couldn't walk nor speak." My mother shook her head then calmed herself down. "Well at least him soul find rest."

That was one comfort that we both shared. He was a useless, abusive, drunk in this life but maybe he could be at peace in the grave. I thought this the entire service and even when we stood over the hole in ground, waiting for his coffin to be lowered. A small part of me felt sad, but I couldn't help feeling pleased. There'd be no more beatings, no more cursing, no more him, and all because of me. Well—me and Mama Tulu. The moment I thought of her, I knew she was there among us. I looked up and there she was, standing under an ackee tree ten yards away, her shawl flapping in the air and her umbrella twirling behind her head.

I looked at my mother to make sure she didn't see the obeah woman and sure enough, my mother was so engrossed in lowering my father that she didn't notice anything else. I didn't think that the woman's magic would work, but here we were. "She must want her payment," I thought, but when I looked back, Mama Tulu was gone.

***

The second time I climbed the hill to Mama Tulu's house was much easier than the first. I had to do it in the dead of night again, because God forbid anyone saw me climbing to her house. My mother and I would be outcasts like her. The funny thing is, we all knew that people in the village must have went to her, but nobody knew who. In fact, if it wasn't for Miss Jacob's son, Troy, I'm sure no one would believe in Mama Tulu at all.

Troy Jacobs was a "nasty little ragamuffin" that the whole town hated. He was in and out of Saint Catherine Correctional facility since he was eighteen, and robbed half the people in the town. "Him all yell out nastiness to the likkle gyal picknie on them way to church. Can you believe?" Miss Jacklyne told my mother a few weeks after we moved back to the parish. "Well, him make a sad mistake one day ah market."

Apparently Troy had stolen a jackfuit from Miss Jacklyne's stand and ran right into Mama Tulu, knocking her into the ground. "Move yuh rotten saul from front ah me!" he yelled then ran off.

Mama Tulu gathered herself and didn't say a word, but that was the last that anyone ever saw of Troy Jacobs. Well, not exactly the last. A bunch of people claimed to see him in the dead of night, wondering through the village. "Yeah mon, she tun him into one ah 'ar Nameless." Miss Jacklyne said. "Him wonder ah night time, eyes white as a bed sheet, and gather all di tings wheh she need fi do 'ar dark deeds and spy pon people fi 'ar." She leaned in closer and her voice dropped to a whisper. "She even lay with di bwoy when heat take 'ar."

I'd never met Troy because all of this supposedly happened before we moved back, but his fate sounded terrible. To be some obeah woman's slave for the rest of his life? I wouldn't wish that on anybody.

Again, I saw the tiny light of Mama Tulu's oil lamp ahead of me. I had all of my savings with me. Dear God, I hope it's enough. She never told me how much all of this would cost. After she licked my palm she sent me on my way and I was too happy to get away from her. I tried not to show it, but the woman gave me chills.

Once at her house, I tapped gently at her door. A few moments later she opened it. Her hair wasn't in a braid but fell in curly white tresses around her shoulders.

She stared at me, confused. "Back again? Don' tell me yuh wan kill off yuh maddah now?" She moved to the side and welcomed me in.

"No, I-I came to pay you." I stepped into her house then looked in my bag and pulled out the jar I kept my money in. I extended the jar to her, but Mama Tulu only looked at it.

"Payment? Yuh already pay me."

Now it was my turn to be confused. "What d you mean? I never gave you any money."

She laughed. "Money is not di only way to pay gyal. Yuh give me permission over yuh bloodline. Yuh give, an' me take."

A creak in the floorboards in the back startled me, but after looking around I saw nothing. I turned back to Mama Tulu. "What do you mean? I didn't give you permission for anything."

"Yes, yuh did. Yuh gave away yuh blood. Yuh said yuh want him to go away. Just so happen me need another set ah helpin' hands around here."

The cold feeling returned and washed over me. My hands went clammy, but the palm of my hand stung as it hadn't since the night Mama Tulu pricked me. The floorboard creaked again. And again. I didn't want to turn around. I didn't want to face what I had done, but I could feel him standing there behind me, his breath hot on my neck. Slowly I turned, and looked into the deep brown eyes that once brightened in the sun, now glazed over and white.

WHEN THE MOON FELL DOWN

L. Lark

L. Lark is a secret toad,
living amongst humans in
Portland, OR.

"We ran as if to meet the moon." ~ Robert Frost

Jone has suspected the moon is moving closer since her first night out of the hospital.

This is not confirmed until several evenings later, from the pier. It is January, and blood oranges arrive in crates from the southern territories. Acidic air whittles at the pier's ancient planks, and even pelicans have fled, unable to find suitable perch. In moonlight, the bare masts of ships unloading in the dock remind Jone of an enormous tree, struck by lightning.

Jone is grateful to be working again, despite the oranges. Their juice burns the skin beneath her fingernails, and the men who come to collect crates in the morning never seem to have awakened from dreams of the night before. But this is winter, Jone knows, when dreams are thickest, and the oranges arrive to remind them the sweet, warm wind of the south has long to travel before spring.

Across the bay, the lighthouse continues to sweep its eye across the water. It is the only relic that remains from old Odeliza, in its years before the fire. Jone's ancestors built the lighthouse, just as they reconstructed Odeliza from its ashes, but Jone has only been to its top twice, but the final time had not ended well.

This is why no one notices the moon is too close, Jone

reasons, but the proximity of its pockmarked crust makes her uneasy.

***

In the morning, Jone rows out to see Erba, the witch.

Erba lives on a slender island where the bay narrows into a river. Erba is another word for hare, which is another word for moon, and she has two white dogs that snap at Jone's oars as she maneuvers her rowboat onto the beach.

"I told you not to come back here," Erba says from the tide-line. There is kelp spiraled around Erba's ankles, but her dress is unstained. Erba wears a shoot of coral around her neck, and its orange is that of the sun draining color before night.

"I need to ask about the moon," Jone calls, and Erba's dogs yelp and cough and spit foam onto the white sand. Overhead, two gulls narrowly escape collision.

"You're worrying," Erba says, knowing Jone cannot ignore things like unexpected weather, or early bird migrations. "Best not to worry about the moon. I'm sure she was just tired of the view."

They drink bitter hawthorn tea in Erba's cabin, while the dogs chew on a pair of soup bones beneath the table. The home is small and dark, like Erba. The gold thread weaved into her braids glints in a narrow steam of light from eroded wood in the rafters.

Erba stands a head shorter than Jone, but she has thick hair and thighs and fingernails, and gives the impression of great density.

Jone is tall and can hoist crates of fruit from the ships without assistance. Jone's hair is copper, but her fair complexion suggests the influence of some vague and untreatable illness. The crook of her left arm is still bruised from the nurses' injections, so Jone stirs tea with her right, and hopes Erba will choose not to mention Jone's long absence.

"The moon is getting closer," Jone begins, but Erba lifts a hand to interrupt. Erba has always preferred gestures to speech, and when Erba does talk, it is most often with a hand over her mouth, as if she is afraid the words might charge forward too quickly.

Erba is able to light a candle at the table's center, despite her damp matchbook. The plump flame illuminates conch shells on the mantle.

"I told you not come to back here. Drink your tea before the tide comes in, would you? I have to feed the chickens," Erba says, with her face turned so that Jone cannot see her mouth.

"But the moon —"

"Will do as she pleases. If you're worried, I can make you a charm to keep in the pocket of your coat. It will be a gull's foot, so keep it hidden, or they will want to send you back to the doctors."

Jone is careful to keep her expression neutral. She takes a sip of tea, and her glasses fog. Erba's cabin has always smelled soft and damp, and Jone suspects she is allergic to the bright yellow mold spreading in the corners.

Jone coughs into the crook of her arm.

"I understand," Jone says, and tries to stop looking at the fine black shadows cast by Erba's eyelashes. For a moment, Jone has the terrible feeling that some sentence has been omitted from their conversation, and Jone will never know what it is.

"I can take care of the moon myself, but give me the charm, in case."

***

The first Odeliza burned in its entirety, and was rebuilt by priests of the Four Hundred Gods. Their missionaries had arrived on whaling boats, which paused in Odeliza to restock fresh water and canned fruits as they followed pods on their migratory route north.

Odeliza's old churches had scorched alongside its canneries, and brothels, and smokehouses, and the missionaries brought gods to replace those destroyed by the flames. They'd rebuilt Odeliza with white rock from vast quarries in the foothills, which had once been the sacred land of whatever had existed here before men.

Jone was born in Odeliza, as was her mother, and her grand-mother, and the cats in the alleys of her childhood apart-ments, descendants of those who'd escaped the fire a century before. Jone's father was from the foothills, and when Jone was young, he'd wandered into dense white fog squeezing through a mountain pass and never returned.

Jone's mother never spoke of him.

"This city is your father. Your ancestors built these roads. Before you were born, I carved your face into a stone from the quarry, and you emerged an exact replica," Jone's mother assures her, while stirring chunks of crabmeat into a stew of pureed rice. The steam feels too thick to breath. "Your bones are made of white rock."

Jone's surname is Aile, which means eel in the language of the missionaries. Everywhere, the silhouettes of these slender fish are stamped into bricks and above doorways. Jone has never thought about this very deeply. There are many Ailes in Odeliza. The missionaries had not only distributed their gods, but their surnames as well.

However, Jone quietly wishes her mother were right. She lifts a pool of stew into her mouth with bread crust. Even in the fundamental familiarity of her childhood home, Jone has felt lost for quite some time.

Later in life, Jone will sometimes find herself in strange parts of the city with no memory of how she's traveled there. The night she is taken to the hospital, Jone steals a dinghy from the docks and smashes it against the boulders of Lighthouse Island. She does not recall any of this, but when she is arrested in the lantern room, Jone has already been screaming into the sky for some time.

***

By the following evening, everyone in Odeliza is whispering, in pubs and on the docks and behind stacks of overripe fruit at the market. The air is pulpy, and sticks to the roof of Jone's mouth, but this is easy to ignore with the moon the way it is.

"You're not needed today," says Jone's overseer at the docks. He does not turn to face her as she approaches from the muddy road that connects the bay to her small room at the boarding house. Jone has a hand pressed into her abdomen, which aches dully from black coffee served on the ground floor of her building. It had been difficult to sleep with moonlight burning through her curtains.

"The ships can't get in or out of the bay. The tides have gone mad. Oh, you know what I mean, Joney, don't look so offended."

The docks are crowded with sailors and fishermen, but all seem frozen mid-movement. Even the seal colony is silent, aside from the occasional crack of a yawning jaw.

Odeliza is small, and its houses are crooked, and its year is marked by what arrives from the ships; oranges in winter, lavender in spring, apples in the fall. Before her time in the hospital, Jone had sometimes worked on the boats, and sailed to places with one temperature and palm fronds that slapped against one another in the wind, but that was before — before everything.

"I have an idea of what to do," Jone says, dropping a hand

from her abdomen to her pocket, where Erba's charm seems to twitch. Erba's magic always has a nervous, impatient sense to it.

"Is anyone listening? I've known this was coming for some time. The moon has been sending us warnings," Jone continues.

No one seems to notice her.

***

It was eight months ago that Jone first attempts to tell Erba there is something peculiar about the moon. In the city, horse hooves pound on cobbled streets, and the trees have not yet begun to bear their slender bones.

This is before Erba asks Jone to leave the island and not return. It is nearly spring, and flowering trees make Jone sneeze into the crook of her arm. Erba's dogs roam the tall grass, searching for fledgling birds that have tumbled from their nests.

Jone is sore from her work on the docks, but Erba insists they follow the dogs, so Erba can gather holy basil in the island's meadow. On this day, the sky is orange. The sunlight is filtered and weak through a haze of pollen.

This important, Jone knows, but light is such an easy thing to ignore, especially in the weeks before the moon moves closer. Jone has never before paid attention to highlight and shadow and shade. After the moon comes, she sees nothing else.

Jone reaches for Erba's hand, and finds it clutched around a bushel of lavender. Erba's fingernails are pale and violet, but her body heats the air around it. When they had first met, Jone had asked Erba how she'd become a witch and Erba had said: "When I was a child, I fell into a well in the olive groves, and in it found a perfect sphere of white stone, which I felt compelled to swallow for luck. No one saw me fall. I spent the evening in the well with the stone glowing in my stomach, and in the morning, my body floated back to the surface. The robins were singing and I could understand every word."

They had not spoken of it then, but every child in Odeliza understood that after the great fire, the city had been rebuilt from white rock unlike any other in the mountains. Before the Four Hundred Gods had forbidden such thought, it was common knowledge the rocks had fallen from the sky.

"I have something to tell you," Jone says later, after they have steeped the lavender and basil into sweet, fragrant water. "I've been receiving messages from far away."

Erba looks back to Jone from her place over the stovetop. Steam winds through Erba's curled hair. "Say that again, would you, darling? I don't think I understood."

"The moon is speaking to me," Jone says, feeling as though a secret compartment inside of her has been shattered. Jone holds on to physical sensations — the soreness in her shoulders, an old injury in her left knee that aches in certain weather. When the moon whispers, Jone feels as though she is floating directly above her own body.

Erba stares back at Jone. Erba's hair is dense and shining. The cabin is full of magic, always, but it seems absent now, in the truthful light of afternoon. Erba only ever kisses Jone at dawn, and then again at twilight. Every kiss Jone remembers as having a certain color and weight, like jewels.

"You've said a lot of strange things lately. Perhaps you don't need a witch. Perhaps you need a doctor, " Erba states, which is the last thing she will say to Jone for some time. There is a windstorm blowing in from the south and the island smells of crab, soon to be washed ashore.

Jone pinches the bridge of her nose, though Erba's potion has already eased her headache.

In the present, life has paused. During the day, people are moved to speak in hushed voices, but nights are silent, aside from the trill of crickets, unmoved by the vast white landscape overhead. By mid-week, silver dust falls continuously from the sky, like rain. People pull scarves over their mouths, afraid to breath the moon's shedding skin.

Jone runs out of money, like everyone else. She drinks coffee at the boarding house and eats plain rice at the church and finishes off her prescriptions. The withdrawal takes three days, and after, even when Jone has stopped tasting copper, the muscles in her lower back clench at odd moments.

By then, the moon is close enough to fill the sky. Jone sees her neighbors glancing desperately to the last navy slit crescent along the horizon. Like everyone else in Odeliza, Jone spends every evening on the sidewalks, but less because of the moon, and more because her bed sheets have begun to stink and she feels lightheaded at all times.

***

Erba can name all Four Hundred Gods, but does not believe in any one of them. This is something Erba insists Jone understand clearly. Erba's allegiances still lie with old spirits of the fishing line, of high tide, of the gibbous moon.

"Don't speak of this off the island. They've sent me here because they are afraid of me, but they are not afraid of you."

There was a time before the Four Hundred when the moon had her own name and her own feast and her own priests. Erba says she remembers which herbs will make the moon speak, so Jone helps Erba gather fennel and almonds from the greenhouse. The weeds turn Jone's hands splotchy and pink, but she obeys Erba's militaristic commands.

Jone's heart gives odd vibrations between its normal beats,

but it's good to work again, and feel the calluses on her fingers scrape against thorns on the rosebush.

Erba instructs Jone to drop what she has gathered into a boiling pot of water on the stovetop. It emits a smell that reminds Jone of aluminum, and singes the hairs inside her nose. It is a day of discomfort, in all senses, but Jone finally feels like she is occupying her own body.

"My molars hurt," Jone tells Erba happily, and Erba knows to ignore this statement.

"Careful, you'll burn yourself. We're going to use them to talk to her. Or rather, to listen, if she decides to speak."

"How does it work?" Jone asks, even though she knows Erba will always decline to explain her spells. Jone has spent her life moving crates and listening to the predictable slap of water against the beach. Jone knows the ocean, but witchcraft is more nebulous.

When the vials have cooled enough to handle, Erba leads them into the island's clearing. Erba fills a silver bowl with brackish water and together, they pour the mixtures onto its surface. Jone is not cold, although she feels she should be.

"What's supposed to happen?" Jone says.

"Some versions of this spell make an enemy's horses go lame. If I had replaced the fennel with toadwort, it would have caused all unmarried women in Odeliza to drown themselves. In this case, it's a trap. If there is a message out there, it will get stuck inside."

Erba speaks little when she does magic, but her fingernails and eyes seem clear and bright. Erba motions for Jone to circle the bowl counter-clockwise four times, then crouch alongside her. They stare into the craters reflected on the liquid's surface.

"It looks like a city," Jone says, finally interrupting the discordant sound of crickets, confused about the time of day.

"Of course, Jone. Sometimes, I forget you were born beneath the Four Hundred."

"As were you," Jone says, feeling as though Erba has meant this statement as an offense, but not sure how.

"Before the Four Hundred, there were roads connecting this world to many others. Even your mother would have been too young to remember that your family helped build those roads, and later, destroy them."

"In the fire?" Jone asks. There are history books in Erba's cabin, but Jone reads at a tortuously slow pace, and there are always dogs to feed and branches to prune and weevils to pluck out of the garden.

"No, some things were destroyed by priests of the Four Hundred. What was left burned. It was sad, a long time ago. Now, it's only history. Oh. I think we've caught a message."

Jone does not immediately understand what Erba is referring to. The moon hovers closely overhead, reflected in the bowl. Erba pushes her shirtsleeve up to the elbow and reaches into the water.

Erba's hand emerges with what looks like a silver marble. This, she drops onto her tongue and Jone sees Erba's throat bob. After a moment, Erba coughs and beats a fist against her chest. She attempts to pull something from her mouth, but it is only one of Jone's hairs, tossed sideways by the wind.

"Bleh. Salty. In a moment, I will need you to pay attention to every word I say. Remember everything, even if you don't believe it is important."

Erba's dress is too thin for the weather. Jone can see Erba's stomach clenching beneath the fabric.

"When you speak nonsense, it's witchcraft. When I do it, it's madness."

"There are times when you should only listen, Joney."

Jone does, but hears nothing aside from the dogs barking at rats in the cabin. Erba sits quietly for longer than Jone expects her to, but Jone flinches at Erba's every breath, assuming she is about to be frightened.

"Hello," Erba says, finally. It has become either very early or very late. Erba's leather boots groan in the cold.

"Hello," Jone replies, as she realizes that Erba has not instructed her on whether or not to respond. Erba's head falls back, and Jone reaches out to catch Erba's shoulders, but stops short

"I don't mean to startle you. It's only that I've been alone for a long time. On Earth, there are maps, but in space, you are always lost, even when you think you know where you are."

Jone realizes this is Not-Erba. Not-Erba speaks slowly and her voice is thick and sweet, like the drone of bees in summer.

"That is a very frightening thing for you to say," Jone tells Not-Erba. Not-Erba brushes a stray eyelash away from the cup of her cheek. It feels like there is fluid in Jone's lungs.

Not-Erba nods. "But that is not what I am here to tell you, of course, that is something you already know. I am here to gather the pieces of myself that I have left behind, but it's difficult to get so close. You'll have to come the rest of the way."

Not-Erba's words only make sense if Jone is dreaming. She can normally tell she is asleep by the numbers on a clock face, by the alignment of stars, but there are no more stars — the moon has stolen the sky entire.

"Aren't you going to say anything?" Not-Erba asks. "The space around your eyes is red. "

"It means I am sad, and also afraid."

"Why are you afraid? I have been with you for a long time already, in your city and in the belly of your witch."

Not-Erba gives a terse smile, as if she us using only the

muscles of her top lip. It is a difficult expression, and one Jone cannot interpret. Jone watches Not-Erba push the heels of her palms into her eye sockets.

And then, Not-Erba is gone, and it feels as through the ground has exhaled and Jone is sinking into the earth. Erba is coughing dryly into the crook of her elbow. Erba attempts to speak, but her voice is too thin to travel any distance.

"What did she say?" Erba finally manages, through a pair of ill-timed breaths. Behind her, the jagged mountain range across the bay looks like silver.

"We need to get up high," Jone says, then adds, "You always said I could be a witch too. You always said there was only the smallest of steps between madness and magic. Do you believe that, Erba?"

"No, I only said that to distract you," Erba says, "Magic is the opposite of madness. Magic is left behind once all the madness has been cleared away."

***

Along the docks, the masts of remaining ships wobble together. A handful of sailors in yellow raincoats are untying their boat from the hitches, although Jone knows the swells are too dangerous for a vessel its size. There is a grave for every boat at the bottom of the ocean.

"I thought it was raining," Erba laughs, her teeth large and reflective. She has both palms open and is gathering dust that drops from the moon overhead. Her hair and the sad slope of her shoulders are coated in silver.

Jone reaches out and touches the bird bones of Erba's wrist.

"Even if we survive this, I don't know if we will be able to see each other without thinking of the moment when the world nearly ended. The moon will always be between us."

Jone agrees with this, but she presses her mouth against

Erba's anyway. Erba tastes of fennel bulb and fresh tea and magic, and the kiss burns.

"I don't understand your plan." Erba admits, turning her face away.

"Neither do I. This is what the moon told me. She said some words are spells of their own."

"I was the one who told you that, Jone."

"I know. I was just trying to upset you, in hope that you will be less troubled by my next suggestion."

"Which is what, Jone?"

"We're going to get on a boat."

Erba looks from Jone to the rolling green water. Distant lighting strikes the tips of waves, exposing the skeletal frame of sunken ships beneath the bay. Erba hides her face beneath her palm, and Jone knows that Erba wants to be afraid. There is every reason to be fearful of the moon, and none to believe that the moon needs their help.

"This is madness, Jone. We'd be capsized as soon as we left the bay. There are sharks, and they are hungry and we have nothing but soft limbs and skin."

"We don't need to leave the bay. We only need to get there," Jone says, pointing towards the swinging beam of the lighthouse, unattended.

***

The waves seem to combine into faceted, architectural structures. Erba follows Jone's directions with terse movements, and their path is lit by the florescent squid that flee their wake. The dock on the island has dissolved with age, but Erba and Jone are able to guide the boat against what pillars remain, and haul their bodies carefully across the planks to the boulders on the shore.

Jone has heard gossip that the lighthouse keeper fled three nights ago, and the door to the cabin is unhinged. However, two yellow galoshes lay abandoned in the foyer, next to a bucket of live bait that struggles dully in reeking water. The cabin is silent, aside from the deep pulse of a pendulum clock behind a door.

Erba says nothing until Jone finds the trail that leads them to the latched door of the lighthouse proper.

"You've been here before," Erba says, watching Jone attempt to force the handle open. "Move aside, I will ask the lock to open for us."

A gear clicks beneath Erba's palm.

"Yes. I used to bring the keeper crates of flour and evaporated milk from the docks. Once, she took me up the stairs to see the lantern. It was daytime, but there was a faint half-moon above the horizon. It was the first time I ever saw the moon so close."

Jone chooses not to mention her arrest. Erba is already aware, and if she is not, then Jone sees no reason to make her so.

An iron staircase rattles beneath their boots. The great hollow body of the lighthouse smells of mold, and even Jone's shallowest breaths seem to trigger echoes throughout the chamber. Erba's hand does not leave the railing once they pass the second landing. Erba is a witch of tide pools and conch shells and sand. She is terribly afraid of heights.

By the time they've reached the top of the staircase, their breaths sound like a campfire, dying in the morning cold.

The door to the lantern room is unlocked and swings open easily. Jone does not know if the deep vibration she feels is the result of two gravitational forces, pushing against one another.

Jone looks down towards her torso and is surprised to find

herself there, whole and unbroken. "I'm sorry. I feel strange, like my body is stretching in all directions."

"I'll say a blessing for you."

"No. I need to feel it."

"Jone," Erba says, in the same way nurses and doctors have spoken it before, offering pink pills in paper cups.

"Help me onto the ledge."

Jone yawns, as she always does when she is nervous. There is a howling from beyond the door, like hounds on the trail of a fox, but Jone cannot remember any stories about dogs on the moon.

"Oh, Erba," Jone says, as her hand clutches the brass latch that opens to the round balcony outside. "Do you think I've called the moon here by accident? Is this my fault?"

"It may be," Erba agrees, and captures Jone's hand in her own.

The air smells like ash and wax and the cold high tide. The winds here are stronger than on the docks. An iron railing wraps around the lighthouse's top without ornament or ceremony, like the bars of a jailhouse. It reaches only Jone's waist. Any misstep could send them both tumbling into the jagged range of rocks below.

Outside, Erba's skin seems translucent. Jone follows the trail of a blue vein that travels across Erba's forehead and through a cheekbone towards her throat. The old dip of a chickenpox scar on Erba's shoulder fills with shadow. In this light, Erba is brilliant and monumental.

"I thought I might know what to do once I got here," Jone says.

From the west comes the deep rumble of a landslide, but whether it has happened on earth or on the moon, Jone can no longer tell.

"You'll have the strength. Imagine your spine is the root of a tree, anchored into the ground."

"I don't think you understand," Jone says. "A long time ago, you found a white stone at the bottom of a well and you swallowed it, and that is how you became a witch."

Erba is expressionless, but silver bands of light continue to move across her face. Jone looks across the bay to the dark summit of a cloudbank. Along the far horizon, a ship's lantern blinks, then disappears.

Erba does not answer. Jone continues, "I've realized now that the moon is only here because she is missing something. She does not want to harm us. This is the end of a trade."

From behind them, the lantern flares awake like a snap of lightning, and both Jone and Erba clap their hands over their ears. They stumble back, so that the distance between them is blocked off by light.

"I'm afraid I must ask what you mean by that," Erba calls, as if there they are separated by great lengths.

If Jone squints into the light, it creates the illusion of a staircase that rises indefinitely upwards. Jone had hoped that the moon would make it difficult, that her expectations would not be fulfilled, and she would be left alone on the surface of a dark earth. Jone had not wanted a choice. Having a choice means Jone might have the opportunity to make the wrong one.

"The moon was your mother once," Jone says. "This light is not a light. It is a road."

Erba already knows this, of course. Erba has always been the first to see a trail, if there is one. After all, Erba had been the one to find Jone first, years ago. Jone had been trolling the beach for supplies from cargo ships wrecked by a storm in the night. Erba, searching for shards of sea glass, had worn a scallop shell against her chest.

Jone wishes Erba would run, but she doesn't. Erba takes a step forward and dips her fingers into the light. As she does, a pulse seems to travel beneath her skin, like Erba's veins have been refilled with something brilliant and metallic.

"Say something. The moon won't leave without you. You've always said you were tired of the island. The dogs will feed themselves, and the island will feed itself with what the dogs cannot catch. "

"Oh, Joney—"

"She'll kill us all, if you don't. The sailors and the dockworkers, and the merchants, and the cats who steal fish from the market, and the priests, and any other witches who were unlucky enough to be born from a different mother than you were."

"Jone, listen. The moon is not asking for me. She's asking for you. Look," Erba says, pointing up along the staircase. There is salt on Erba's fingernails, shining like scales.

There are carvings on the riser of each step, and Jone recognizes the outline of an eel, an Aile, the stamp of Jone's distant relatives—the same image found on Odeliza's markets and schools, and even at the base of the lighthouse on which they now stand.

"Your family built this road, like they built all others in this city. You were wrong about me, Joney. I was not the sacrifice, I was the bait. Or, at least, that was what the moon intended me to be. The truth is, Jone, I will never be bait. I will always only be a witch."

There are bubbles popping in Jone's stomach. She blinks into the light.

"And above all, witches love the roads that have never been taken. The first step is yours, that I cannot take away from you, but I will follow when you choose to go."

Jone cannot speak, and so the sea speaks instead, through

waves that beat against the edge of the island. The ocean has only ever spoken one word, in all of its infinite lifespan, and that word has been go go go.

"Why do you think she wants me?" Jone says. She is aware that her voice is high and quiet, but Jone knows that Erba will understand. Erba would understand the silent motion of the stars, if by their motion alone they intended to speak.

"Only the moon knows. I don't have every answer." Erba's teeth catch the moonlight when she smiles. "Go on now. I will be behind you. I know a charm that will prevent us from being blinded as we ascend."

There is dull, thudding pain beneath Jone's breastplate. The eels carved into the staircase–the staircase made of rock particles suspended in a beam of light–seem to inhale all at once. Jone wipes her palms against the thigh of her trousers.

Erba follows close behind, but it is Jone who takes the first step towards the sky.

THE OLD HOTEL

Nicole Janeway

I am currently freelancing in
Barcelona, though at the end of
the year I'll move to Washington,
D.C. to work as a consultant.
I love dogs, running in the
mountains, and café con leche.
My writing has appeared in
Cicada and Scarlet Leaf Review.

"The Old Hotel" was previously
published in Scarlet Leaf
Review.

I empathize with this building. It collapses into itself - built of cobwebs and dark, and held upright by the last of our hopes. I drift down the halls and am not alone. There are other figures who wander and seek. What are they looking for? An old shoe, a forgotten secret, a lost love. I do not know. I let these imagined stories of their search fill my thoughts, consciousness seeping outward like fog until the mind is inseparable from the space it inhabits. The building keeps me from drifting off completely. Its creaking and settling are like breathing, inhaling and exhaling once or twice each night. If I cannot remember who I am, it is because my identity is seeping into the floors my feet shift silently over without disturbing a carpet of dust.

There is a partly torn photograph lying by crates of moldy bedding and a curtain that used to hang across the stage. Two people; a suit and a dress. She stands tiptoe on feet that remember dancing. Terpsichoreans blur the backdrop and to the far left light glimmers off instruments belonging to the Bantam Brass Boys. It is a wonder that I know the musicians' name and not my own.

I have wandered that room, I have stood where they stood, laughing, fresh-faced from dancing. It is in the base of this hotel. I am bound to the building and to the photograph, to the girl. I am looking at a familiar face in passing and get a feeling of deja vu. I do not look at the man's face; that pain is for the living.

Tonight I feel a hand on my shoulder. I have forgotten how to touch, how to be touched. It is one of many, but not the most important of the things I have lost. Soft music floats around us, rich and smooth. Jazz has always sounded navy to me. One last dance, I understand.

This could all exist within my own mind, I think, but I look at him and forget. He has the eyes from the picture, gazing out with such earnestness. Lilly, he calls me, and as he says it I can see this place as it once was. The dancing couples around us are revelers in their own living. The talented musicians play over the sound of glasses of bootleg alcohol clinking. Feet I once considered light press against the gleaming wooden floor.

If I had breath to take away, I would have been left gasping by this specter of the past.

It's almost dawn, I want to say, but the words are shadows fleeing the light. They are strangers I will never know. For a moment, I despair. I have had an unwanted excess of time, a parade of nights, and now I have too little, for who knows if this glorious fantasy will exist tomorrow.

He squeezes my hand. How can he steal the air from me? He guides me gently into a dilapidated lobby where jazz music still envelops my ears. He keeps walking toward the doors though I hesitate and my fingers slip. He is a kite spooling to the end of my reach, but after so long letting everything slide away, I hold on. We step into light that laps at us like waves.

WAYFARERS

Heather Morris

Heather Morris is a cyborg
librarian living in North Carolina.
Her work has appeared in Apex
Magazine, Strange Horizons, and
Daily Science Fiction, among
other places. You can find her
on Twitter @NotThatHeatherM

The day of the harbor bombing I was a mile away, but I thought I was done in anyway, 'cause I heard the blasts and then felt something slippin' out my inners. When I ducked behind a building to piss, there was a bright red stain down there, already turnin' brown around the edges, and more and more blood to make sticky my shakin' hands.

Well what course did I have bein' so far away from home as that and the city all wild with the bombs? I ran to Honeycomb, the closest safe place I knew, and begged for Meli. She didn't like gettin' out of bed afore dusk, but it just wasn't the kinda day for lazing. Let into her plush, golden room, I showed her the blood and begged her to get my body to the gang, not let me fall into the hands of organ reapers or the wayfarers.

Blue smoke from her kitaka clouded the air, and she made a snort deep in the back of her throat, the kinda sound I didn't think a classy whore could make.

"You ain't dyin', kiddo, it's just your monthly."

I stared at her, heart still thumpin' like a war drum, but slowin'. Ain't dyin'.

"Monthly what?" I asked.

Well, she 'bout fell into hysterics. When she finally stuttered out what it meant, that I was a woman real and true, I started to howl and didn't think I could ever stop.

For twelve years I figured that one day I would wake up a boy. Bein' a woman was worse than bein' dead.

Meli tapped out the kitaka and crawled from the bed, naked as the day is long. She wrapped some transparent gauze the same shade as her honey-dark hair round her shoulders, knelt before me, and placed an awkward hand on my dusty head, and it was only then that I shut up my trap. The head whore of Honeycomb was not known for her condescension, and until that moment I'd always thought she just saw me as an annoying extension of Cas, but somehow I had been enough to get her out of her famous bed.

"Those boys touch you yet?"

I wasn't stupid enough to pretend I didn't know what she meant. I sniffed up a load of snot. "No ma'am, an' they never would."

Her clear blue eyes turned sad, and then hard, her hand still stroking me like I was a dog. "You'd be surprised how men are, Athena. Don't tell them you've bled."

"They never would," I said again, my voice brittle as glass. I did not like her sayin' my gang could hurt me, not one bit. Those were my brothers.

She sighed, stood. "Oh, kiddo, I hope you're right. I'll get Thais to clean you up. Stay careful of your boys, and remember, stay away from the wayfarers."

"I always stay away from the wayfarers," I grumbled, starin' down at the floor. Meli turned on me, rough as a cat in heat.

"I mean it, Athena, this is not a joke. You know what they do with us, with anyone they think can make babies."

"But I ain't pretty," I protested.

"Their pretty and our pretty...it ain't the same thing. They'll be able to smell the blood, no matter how you try to cover it up, so you remember to stay away from them when it's on you. Far away.

There wasn't so far you could go on the island, never far enough to be out of their reach. But I nodded a promise. At least I would try.

***

Who my parents were, only the gods might know, but I used to pretend they were a great lord and lady, rich and beautiful and favored by the wayfarers, the type of people the bombers meant to attack when they blew up the row house that orphaned me. Probably my mother was a lady's maid who spent her days curling hair and probably my father was a charming scoundrel who offered nothing more than a squirt of sperm, but doesn't everyone like to pretend?

But who I was never really mattered, 'cause either way I woulda ended up where I did which was, at six months of age, on my way to the temple to be sacrificed. The row house attack had been the worst to hit the city since the resistance began, and there weren't resources to care for survivors that couldn't take care of themselves. I would be a blood offering to the wayfarers and the gods, a hopeful appeasement to stop the violence burning the city from the inside.

And that woulda been the end of my story, if not for Cas. He never, not once, told me what he saw in an infant girl that would make him risk life and limb (his two favorite things) to save her, and I ain't never been stupid enough to ask. He was ten years old then, already quite a leader of scavengers. He stole me from under the eyes of the guard, called me Athena for luck, and ever since that day I have belonged to him.

The reason I'm tellin' you all this? Well, I guess it's 'cause, in a way, my life started 'cause of one bombing, and ended 'cause of another. And both the starting and the ending happened 'cause of Cas.

The harbor bombing that day was a big one, and no mistake. There hadn't been a direct attack in the city for years and years, and the harbor was the lifeblood of us all. The wayfarers controlled all the imports and exports. They lived all along the waterfront in their blinky ring houses, keepin' the rest of us in check. I could hear their screechy screams following me all the way home, even as the press and pull of crowds grew. People wanted to watch, people wanted to cause trouble, people wanted to get their hits in before the guard was organized enough to push the little bit of rebellion down. It wasn't safe to be out on the streets, and I tried to make myself as small as I could, sneakin' round the edges of places.

Our row house was as chaotic as the streets. The landlord's dogs were kenneled in the courtyard, baying mournfully and pulling at the length of their leads. The wayfarer's screams made 'em crazy, but if anyone let them off their leads, well, then there'd be no more dogs, would there? Kids baited them, or each other, daring each other to run to the edges of the road, where their caretakers had warned them not to go. The old men who usually gambled on the boards outside on sunny days were helpin' each other drag the boards inside. Some of the women were coverin' the cistern, in case smoke or worse came through. I woulda helped 'em, but most of the women in the house hated me, 'cause I wouldn't act like a girl or look after their kiddos, called me Cas's slut when they knew I would hear it.

I pushed aside our board and went into our room. No one was in, which was nice, 'cause there was this ball of sick rolling inside me and I just wanted to lie down. I could still hear all the mess and noise outside, but here I was safe behind the walls. I grabbed my blanket and found my niche, and lay down tryin' to shut it all out.

I wasn't worried about the boys. Once the bombs had gone off they would scatter, flit around a bit and then come back to the nest, quick as you like.

***

When I opened my gummy eyes, it was full dark. Linos was poking at my shoulder. "Thena. Thena!"

I groaned and my tummy grumbled. "What, fishface?"

Everyone was home, but too quiet. Simonides was tryin' to kindle up the wayfarer lamp we stole the winter before. A devilish thing, that lamp, that shined the brightest light you ever saw, if it ever decided to catch. Kyros and Demon and Hyakinthos were gathered at the table, talkin' soft. And AgAr—Agathon and Argyros, our very own twins—were hunched up together in their niche, faces splotchy and wet.

Well at that I sat up, fast. My sleepy head buzzed. "What is it?"

"You're dyin'," AgAr wailed. It was always hard to tell which one was talkin', so everyone always thought of the two of them as one. "First the bomb, and then Cas, and now you're dyin'!"

I looked down and saw that the blood had gotten fast and come through, and frowned. So much for that secret. But then somethin' they said caught up with me.

"Cas?"

Where was Cas?

Linos looked at me, the stonefruit bobbing in his throat. "Cas got took."

Panic flushed through me. How could Cas, the best of us, get caught? And by who?

Please be the guard. Please be the guard. If it was the guard, if he got picked up bein' too enthusiastic about the riot or drinkin' too hard, he'd be cooling off in a cell somewhere, makin' friends and waitin' for us to show up with coin to spring him.

"Who?" I croaked.

No one was talkin'. Shit, no one was talkin'.

Simonides finally got the damned light kindled. It made everything in the room orange or shadow. Demon, his black hair pulled low over his eyes, was the only one brave enough to finally open his mouth. "Wayfarers."

Hell. All the hells rolled into one. If Cas got took by the wayfarers, it meant he was in a ring house, and if he was in a ring house, he was already good as dead.

I was so afraid, I felt hollow.

"You left him?" I didn't even recognize my voice. "You left him? Who saw him last?"

In the glare of the light, Demon raised his hand. I woulda whacked him, if he weren't three years and six inches bigger than me.

"What could I do?" he groaned, ashamed. "It was all confused. And I knew if I tried to help, I'd get took, and I knew you'd know what to do, so we had to leave him."

Me? The hollow feeling turned to wind, whistling through my empty bones. I saw what they thought. They thought I could save Cas.

Well, maybe I was the best hope. I love my gang, but let's not try to shine a turd. Most of 'em were dumb as piss. If you have any brains at all, any desire to be anything but a follower, you have your own gang by the age of ten. I was youngest, outside of Agathon and Argyros, but I was smartest, outside of Cas. He was trainin' me, he liked to say. Groomin' me up. Like a favorite dog.

They were all lookin' at me. I had to think.

First things first, I went out to the cistern to clean myself up. AgAr tried to follow me, the babies, but I kicked them back inside.

The whole worked reeked of kitaka smoke.

I have always hated the smell of kitaka smoke, nostril-tickling sweet like a damp, rotting flower. It smells like them. But half the island was hooked on the stuff. Either the rioters had broken into the stores to celebrate, or the wayfarers had sacrificed a bunch of their precious weed to get everyone calmed down.

It made me sleepy. I had to think.

When I got back inside, everyone was still starin'. I sat down in the middle of the floor and tried to corral my spiraling thoughts.

"What, exactly, happened?"

"A guard gave him over to one of the wayfarers," Demon said. "I think he said he was hidin' packages that coulda been bombs. But they were takin' everyone, Athena!"

There was no way Cas was part of any resistance. Even if I didn't know his every movement of every day, I knew Cas. He cared about his own pretty skin, and a rotating roster of maids at Honeycomb, and us, his kiddos, in that order. Even though he was just about old enough to remember some of life before the wayfarers, it wasn't a life he mourned or pined for. With or without wayfarers, his life woulda been pretty much the same. He didn't want revenge, and he didn't have high ideals.

There was someone behind the bombings, that was sure. They probably knew Cas, and others, had been taken for it. And maybe they wanted it that way, 'cause it kept them secret and safe.

Our gang had no chance goin' up against the wayfarers alone, not if any of us wanted to make it back alive. We needed allies, and maybe we needed to find out who set the bombs, too. It all seemed too big, too impossible. But if there was a chance, even a little one, I had to grab at it.

***

That night I dreamed about the gods.

I never really believed in the gods, which might sound funny since I was named after one of 'em. But they didn't feel real—or, if they had been real, I think the wayfarers killed 'em. But that night I dreamed about them all up on their mountain, eating olives and grapes. Just mouths and teeth and olives and grapes.

First thing I did when I woke up was send Kyros to the olive groves and Simonides to the wine merchants. Linos I dispatched to the Guardpost to put his ear to the ground and find out where Cas and the other prisoners were held.

Hyakinthos wanted a task too, so I sent him up to Meli to ask for help. Not that I thought she would, mind. But whores know people, lots of people, so maybe she'd put a word in for us with some of the bigger, braver, or stupider men who patronized her. Demon was the best second, even if I was mad at him, and AgAr were scared, so I kept them with me.

Our job was to go out callin'. We walked down to where the Dog Tooth gang lodged and I stood in the courtyard, all the time thinking I am a woman now, tryin' to look big, and shouted out that we wanted a parley, and where to meet. Same across the city with the Black Rats. Then Apollinarias's crew. Along the way, Demon gathered up men and boys and even some girls who had winesick heads from a night spent protesting and looked like they knew how to use a weapon or two.

Last was Diokles, the Nine Fingers, the biggest hero or biggest drunk on the island, dependin' on who sang the song. It was said he'd been inside a ring house once. Didn't know if it was true or not, but what better person to lead a resistance? Maybe, I thought, he knew where to find the black powder that made bombs.

One of his minions, a wiry little cross-eyed kiddo, came into the courtyard and told me to stop my bellowin'.

"Tell your master to come to amphitheater to parley."

"Parley?" He tasted the word in his mouth and didn't like it. "What for?"

'Cause I think he got us into this mess to start with, I thought but didn't dare say.

"Diokles Nine Fingers is legendary." I tried to take on the cast of a bard. "Today I am making a legend."

The cross-eyed kiddo burst out laughin'. Even AgAr started to snort, and I cuffed one of 'em on the back of the head. Yeah, it had been a dumb thing to say, but how else was I to convince someone that people sang about?

"The wayfarers took people last night," I started again.

"The wayfarers take people all the time. Forget 'em and go find a blind man willing to poke you!"

"What, like you, Cross-Eyes?" I growled. My blood was hot. "Wayfarers take me first!"

He flung his hands over his heart in mock agony and stumbled back. "Tell Upstart Cas to stop sending his minions to do his work. We won't parley with someone who sends girls while he sets a trap."

"They took Cas," I said. "And One-Eyed Anaxagoras. And dozens of others. Men. When was the last time wayfarers took men?" I let that sink into his thick head a bit, then folded my hands in front of my chest. "They have taken too many this time. Tell the Nine Fingers we need him. We will be at the amphitheater. And if he is too groggy-headed to leave his bed, tell him there will be much wine."

I turned on my heel and smiled to myself, thinking, I am a woman.

**

Long, long ago, before they ever came to our shores, the way-farers lost the knowledge of how to make babies. It seems a stupid thing to lose, everyone knows how to do that, but one day it just stopped workin' for 'em. And so they came for us.

Not at first, mind. At first they let us be awed by their big blinky ships that hung in the sky. They taught us their clicky, screechy tongue. They towered over us like gods, and brought all kinds of shiny new trade. Medicine. Technology. This was all before I was ever born, but I know the stories same as everyone. I know what they gave us, and what they took away.

After a time, when we had become used to the wayfarers, they stopped letting us sail. They took over the harbor, and said they were in all other cities, all other places, all around the world. We didn't know if it was true or not. They wouldn't let us leave to find out.

And then they started taking women.

Even after years and years of it, no one knows quite what the wayfarers do. No one comes out alive to tell. Corpses show up once in a while on the beach, piecemeal and unrecogniz-able, picked over by seabirds. There are other corpses with them, sometimes. Scaly, eyeless little halflings. Humanish babies with no mouths to cry. The wayfarers are beautiful, but the things they try to make with us are anything but.

The resistance started with those bodies. We tried to use their own technology, their black powder, to hit their ships that had turned into houses. They put down those upris-ings quick, and the resistance moved on to other humans, those who were seen as colluders. That did not go over well. But still the resistance kept on, until one day the wayfarers emerged from their houses, sent away those who had become their guard, and started roundin' up men.

When we saw those corpses, the resistance stopped for good. As far as an unimportant girl like me had known, anyhow.

As I sat in the bright, hot bowl of the amphitheater, I tried to puzzle out what had started it again.

"Why are we meeting here?" Linos whined, helpin' the others roll in barrels.

'Cause it was the only place big enough for all the people I hoped would come. 'Cause the wayfarers never ventured so far from the sea during daylight. 'Cause there were easy spots to post lookouts, and if anyone saw a guard coming, we could fall on him quick.

I ignored Linos and kept on tryin' to think.

Cas had done lots of favors for the wine merchants over the years, and I called them all in now, and then some, until we had barrels and barrels to offer the crowd. Wine and kitaka are 'bout the only things that get people in the city motivated, and I didn't have any of the weed.

As for the olive growers? Well, I'd heard a rumor once that their guild kept hold of the secret of the Fire, our best weapon before the wayfarers came, which had once been made with one of their cunning oils. I was hopin' to ring it out of 'em.

Apollinarias's crew showed up first, with fish to offer to the communal meal. The Dog Tooth gang came with their signature axes strapped to their sides. No sign of the Black Rats. The stragglers we'd picked up across the city were not impressive in number or stature, and only wanted wine to chase their hangovers. But Apollinarias and the Dog Tooths. That was something, maybe better than I'd hoped.

I came up with a whole speech, but I made Demon say it. No one wanted to hear an ugly girl preachin' about goin' against the wayfarers. Demon was tall and well-spoken and near fifteen. I didn't think the speech would work, mind. But I wanted Cas back, so bad. The pit of my stomach was on fire with hate. And this was the only path I could see.

Men are a lot like boys, and they like to argue and throw fists at one another. Soon enough my proposal for a rescue mission turned into a crazy plan for an assault, and everyone wanted to lead it. So the arguin' grew louder and knottier, and the fists looked like to turn into full brawls, and I figured the whole thing was gonna fall apart before it started.

Then a bright voice rang clear across the amphitheater. "Why don't you speak, girl?"

I looked up, shading my eyes against the sun. Diokles Nine Fingers stood there, a woman at his side.

His minions, Cross-Eyes among them, scampered down the steps of the amphitheater, and Diokles Nine Fingers took the woman's elbow and led her slowly down after them. She was wrapped in white, holding a small parasol to shade her skin from the sun. I gawped. It was Meli.

"I think she's started enough trouble," Meli said, acidly. "Didn't I tell you to stay away from the wayfarers, kiddo?"

I swallowed, desperately. "Don't see any wayfarers here, do you?"

Diokles Nine Fingers chuckled.

He was the handsomest man I ever saw. Brown skinned and wide shouldered with a two-tooth gap in his smile and soft, soft gold eyes. I imagined him touching my skin with his four-fingered right hand—where had that come from?—and a bitter taste shuddered onto the back of my tongue.

"Didn't I say she had a tongue on her, Mels?" he said to Meli, who was pale and furious. Then he turned his attention to me. "You woke me up with your screamin' in my courtyard, girl. So, since I've dragged my ass all the way out here on this shitstain day, why don't you tell me what for?"

I stuttered out the plan, locked in place by his spell-casting eyes.

When I was done, he looked around the amphitheater. "You want to go up against the wayfarers? Truly?"

I shrugged. "All I care about is gettin' Cas back. The ship with blue lights, that's where everyone says they took the prisoners." It was the men who wanted to make something bigger out of it.

"Upstart Cas? Kiddo, no one is here for him. No one likes that schemer."

"I like him," Meli and I protested, in unison.

A smile tugged at the corner of his mouth like an eager fishhook. "No one likes Upstart Cas except for little girls and indulgent whores. And most people are too smart to go against the wayfarers in broad daylight. Yet somehow you managed to get all these people here for a little bit of free wine?"

My teeth ached, I was so on edge with his voice. I looked down at the dust. "There's food, too."

He laughed again, a great, belly-rolling laugh. "Honey, you got a spark. If I'da known Cas was hidin' someone as interesting as you, I might have been paying attention to him all these years."

Meli was not as amused. She looked down at me with her lips pressed tight together. "Athena, I'm sorry about Cas. I really am. He was a sweet boy. But he's dead, and this is dangerous."

"I gotta do something. You don't understand. The wayfarers never took nothin' from you."

"Of course they've taken stuff from me, you little fool. But I don't go around hatching battle plans out in the open where anyone can hear!"

I stared up at her, tryin' to look at things the way Cas would want me to see them. What she was really sayin'. And when I got it, it hit me like a fist.

Meli never left Honeycomb. She had dozens of girls and servants to run her errands, didn't like to dirty her feet with the city streets. But she had come here today. She was tryin' to make out like she was concerned about me, when it didn't make sense that she would care. She didn't want me doin' what I was doin', and it wasn't for my own safety.

"You planned the bombing," I said.

She sucked in a breath. "Don't talk about things you don't understand, Athena. You're just a girl."

I stretched my spine tall. "You planned the bombing. Did you get Cas to help? I don't think he'd be so stupid for anyone but you."

"Cas wasn't involved. I don't know why they took him."

"But it was you."

"If I say yes, will you shut your mouth?"

I could see it now, clear as the sea. Meli and her girls were about the only women in the city who didn't live in constant fear of bein' taken by the wayfarers. They had struck some sort of deal, ages ago. And so under the wayfarer's noses they could meet with men, all kinds of men, and they could talk, and they could plot.

I didn't care about why. I cared about how.

"Then you can help us," I said. "You know where the black powder is!"

"No, Athena, I know where the black powder was. We had a guard on our rolls, but he was taken yesterday with the others, and the wayfarers are sure to have moved it by now."

Diokles grabbed hold of the cup that was bein' passed around and tipped back a swig of wine. "Hittin' the rings now won't get you much of anything anyway. Most all of 'em will be in the one you mentioned, with the blue lights."

"We can make 'em homeless!" a short, stocky man declared excitedly. "Get rid of all the rings they ain't in!"

"And then, what?" Diokles sneered. "You want 'em movin' in with you?"

"The rings are protected anyway," one of the Dog Tooths added. "They have those…what are they called? Fields, all around 'em."

"What you need is a way to get people in," Diokles said. "They're all consumed with the men prisoners right now. You need a distraction, to get their attention off 'em, and get a rescue party inside."

Meli's fingers clenched and unclenched in the empty air. "Nine Fingers, you snake, you ain't supposed to be encouragin' 'em. You said you'd help me knock sense in 'em!"

"Thought I would. But your way didn't work, Mels. And if we can't strike 'em all down this time, well maybe we can at least get a good hit in."

Fury did not sit well on her. Her skin splotched over like a rash and she growled in the back of her throat. She turned away from Diokles.

"Any girl here who wants sanctuary at Honeycomb, come with me now. Let these men come up with their suicidal plots on their own."

She was afraid, and who could blame her? The reprisals, whether we succeeded or failed, would be terrible. She must have seen some sort of gain to be had in the harbor bombing, but that had gone wrong, and now there was no way to win.

But maybe there were better ways to lose. Ways that meant something.

Meli reached for my arm and tugged, half pulling it out of the socket. I tugged back. "I ain't goin' with you."

"Stop," Meli said. "Just stop this. Cas would want you to be safe."

"Cas would want me to fetch him," I retorted. A terrible idea was hatching in my head. The stupidest, most terrible idea I'd ever had.

"I'll be the distraction," I said.

Every eye in the place turned on me then, and I shook under the weight of it all. "I…I…they will know I am a woman. Even with men prisoners, they always want women. I will be the distraction."

***

At least in the end, I wasn't sacrificing myself alone. Two older girls, Korinna and Gaiane, offered to go with me. They were both sallow-skinned and underfed, tall and raw and ugly as me, and I had no idea why they would do such a thing. But some things you just know not to ask.

Meli was havin' a fit, used to dictating what others would do, but the three of us stood firm together. We would try to lure the wayfarers away from their prisoners, as far away as we could before we were caught, and the men would attack. There was no black powder and, to my dismay, no Fire either, but they had axes and clubs and strong hands. And it turned out they had no second thoughts about using weak girls as live bait, which I was kinda hopin' they might.

Even my gang didn't seem too cut up about it. They were psyching themselves up to get Cas, and none of 'em so much as looked my way to say goodbye.

Stupid boys.

Near dusk, Korinna took one of my hands, Gaiane the other, and together we walked down to the harbor.

The only grown women you ever saw down by the ring houses were the desperate ones—streetwalkers lookin' to entice on-duty guards—or old grandmothers. A few months ago, I'd come home glowin' with pride for a particularly good market haul I'd taken in. Cas counted out the spoils, smilin' big as you like, but later that day he'd looked at me, and his eyes burned holes in my skin.

"Athena, no more market for a while, yeah?"

I know my face fell, 'cause I didn't know what I had done wrong. But Cas just rubbed my shoulder and smiled, only this time the smile looked like chipped paint.

Now I knew why. He saw I was gettin' too old. No one ever tells you not to walk the streets alone or to stay away from certain places, not precisely. You just know it. And no one ever tells you why, either. Probably 'cause it makes you feel sick at your own body, the way I did now.

The harbor was grey and cold, empty. The only thing that broke the grey was the lights of the ring houses, blinkin' in patterns. The wreckage from the bombs and their aftermath had not been cleaned up yet. Wood and cloth from the market stalls lay everywhere in piles; the road was pitted and marked.

"We're lookin' for our brother," I reminded the others. I was proud of this little bit of the plan, this reason three girls would be wanderin' 'round the wreckage when they should be smart enough to stay away. They nodded and clutched my hands tighter, 'til our skin was hot and damp pressed together.

"Cassander!" Gaiane called, when we were close enough. "Cassander, darling, please come home!"

Then all three of us were off, wailin' and teary-eyed,

pretendin' to search for a lost little boy who could be buried in the wreckage or hidin' in some hole.

We roused the Guardpost first, as I thought we would. The guards yelled at us to shut our traps, and one even tried to chase us off, but we circled closer and closer to the water, and the rings, and eventually, behind us, their voices stopped. We had not really come alone, after all, and if there's one thing people hate more than wayfarers, it is guards, who betray the rest of us every day for tarnished bits of coin.

I knew they were gettin' the life choked out of 'em just behind me, but I didn't turn to see. I kept walkin' closer and closer to the lights, closer than I ever should have dared, callin' "Cassander! Cassander, dear!" Please be alive to hear, I prayed inside my head. Please be alive to hear and know it is me callin' for you.

And finally, finally, we found our way to the ring house with the blue lights, the biggest, scariest ring house the wayfarers had. And we cried and cried and cried until the door opened wide.

Our chain of hands fell apart, and we scattered.

There's only so far you can run when you are human. Only so far you can run with a bloody cramp in your inners and shaky legs and a stomach empty of anything but bile. But that turns out to be pretty far.

For a minute, or an hour, there was only the slap of my feet on stone, the hot push of air through my lungs. I knew they were there, right there, behind me, and oh my gods I wanted to turn and see 'cause they were so beautiful and I'd never once been so close, but all I could do was run and breathe and run.

Not for long enough, of course. It was never gonna be for long enough.

***

Everyone knows the songs of that night, now, the songs about
rising up for good and all. Songs that taste of the ash on
the air, the salt on our skin. Songs of how the hero Diokles
slaughtered one wayfarer for each of his fingers. Songs of how
six of our boys or men died for every one of theirs. Songs of
how Upstart Cas turned out to be alive after all, and remembered that wayfarer houses were once ships, and that all ships
could sink. Songs of how an army of women, led by the best
of all whores, came to save their stupid, reckless menfolk, and
ended up changing the whole damn world.

I don't get to be part of the songs, unless someone, somewhere, sings of three girls who ran away with the wind while
men and wayfarers first fell upon one another.

But I can tell you three things I learned that night that you
will not hear in songs.

The inside of a ring house is bright metal; the smoothest,
brightest metal you ever saw, and colder than a winter sea.

Wayfarer hands are even colder than that.

And their blood smells the same as ours.

I spent most of that night, the night everything changed,
chained to a wall in a ring full of red lights. Korinna had
been caught with me, but she had slammed her head back
against the smooth metal until she bled, and I might as well
have been alone. The wayfarers hadn't done much more than
chain us up, 'cause they had realized what was really going on
before they had the chance to get started, but soon enough
they would be back, and I had plenty of time to imagine
those cold hands on my skin.

For hours I listened to the soft slap of waves against the
hull. The screams of men, the screech of wayfarers. I smelled
blood—Korinna's, and my own. And I waited, and I waited,
until I realized that no one was ever gonna come for me.

It turns out is just possible, if you are a small girl who has spent her life underfed, to pop the bones in your hand until you can wiggle it out of a tight metal cuff. It is just possible to break someone else's bones, if they are unconscious and can't hate you for it, if it is to save their life. It is just possible to drag an unconscious girl through a maze of cold metal halls, while bright lights pop and blink in your face.

It's possible for the world to change so much in one night that you will never recognize it again.

My best friend drowned taking a ship to the bottom of the sea. My home burned. And the wayfarers kicked us down, but for the first time in my life, we kicked right back.

"Oh, Athena, you're done in now," I whispered into the dark, when I'd gotten myself free. And I found I didn't want any of this, I didn't want it at all. But there was no turnin' back from what was, and I took a deep breath and started towards the fray.

ATTRITION

Leslie J. Anderson

Leslie's writing has appeared in Asimov's, Apex, Strange Horizons, and Daily Science Fiction. Her poetry has been nominated for a Pushcart, Elgin, and Rhysling Award.

Her collection of poetry, An Inheritance of Stone, was recently released form Alliteration Ink and she has a collection of story prompts from Sterling Press entitled 100 Prompts for Science Fiction Writers.

She lives in Ohio with her husband and two small dogs, Caper and Oscar. For her day job she organizes words and pictures for financial consultants.

Anton waved to his grandmother from the freight elevator. She waved back, standing at the edge of the sea of humanity that filled the military warehouse from wall to wall. They were bent, shaking from the rain and fear, desperately trying to shuffle into the correct line for evacuation. His grandmother, Mrs. Anna Louise Christina Pauley, was holding a small, green suitcase with everything she owned. In her arms, she cradled one of the horrible kittens she kept on shelves around the living room. They looked nothing like real kittens, more like a squashed kitten that had been hastily reconstructed through vague description. His grandmother told him, proudly, that they are made from real fur. Anton always wondered where the fur came from.

On the far wall were the ships, though all he could see were the massive, brushed-silver doors where men in uniforms let people through a few at a time. No one was left behind, no matter how sick or old – not today. Everyone was humanity today. Beside them, the last of the Gen 2s, the 100-foot tall battle mechs, waited for their last orders. From the elevator, Anton could barely make out their pilots from where they stood on tall scaffolding next to their sleeping giants. They were hunched slightly, probably from the implant in their spine that let them connect with the half-biological, half-robotic fighting machines. Most of them looked down, somberly, at the mass of humanity underneath them. Everyone had probably lost a friend by now. Quickly, Anton looked back at his grandmother just in time to see her smile.

The fake kitten's glass eyes watched the elevator rise into the ceiling and disappear. Anton wished he could have thought of a better way to say goodbye – something sweet or heroic. Maybe it was best if she thought she would see him again.

Then Anton was alone with the four other people and Diana, the perfectly coiffed and stern-looking woman who pulled them out of the crowd. She had a tablet in her hand and was poking at the screen with increasing concern. Her hair was impeccable, tied tight behind her head. Her suit was simple, expensive. Her makeup was perfect, except for the grey shadow of eyeliner under her eyes, probably from a short cry earlier in the day. Everyone had one.

Anton was taller than her by almost a foot. He was always an awkward height, thin with a black beard he enjoyed growing to a point so he could tug at it when he was thinking. The other people, who all handed their luggage to their families and followed the woman into the freight elevator when their names were called, stood uncomfortably in a ring around Diana. There was a middle-aged man, rotund and balding with a White Lake Football jersey and his hands in the pockets of his jeans. There was a young, redheaded woman in a wheelchair. She stared at the ground with a fury that was almost unsettling. Pamela was the name Diana called her. There was a girl who looked about 16 and a young man who might have been in college. They were holding hands in the back of the elevator, though Anton didn't think they knew each other a few moments before. There was also a uniformed officer with an automatic weapon in his hands.

The building shook and the freight elevator jumped. The five of them stumbled, except Pamela, who rolled a little. Below them, Anton heard people cry out.

"Did they break through?" the man in the jersey asked nervously.

"No, Mr. Henderson. This is the most secure location on the

planet. It will take quite awhile longer to break through," Diana answered dryly.

"But they will?" Anton asked.

"That's why we're evacuating?" the young man asked. "Where are we going?"

"To a secondary location," Diana answered.

"Why weren't we ready?" Mr. Henderson said.

"It was a multi-pronged attack," she said. "Most major cities were lost in three hours."

Mr. Henderson scoffed. "Ridiculous. Unacceptable." He turned his anger unexpectedly toward Anton. "Didn't join up, huh? I suppose you're happy now. It's because of shits like you that this happened."

Out of the corner of his eye, Anton saw the young man shift uncomfortably. The girl leaned against him. Anton had actually checked the 'caretaker' box on the form, because Mrs. Anna Louise Christina Pauley could not always be trusted to find her way down the stairs, or take her pills. He knew the neighbors whispered to her that she ought to make him go, and the Widows and Orphans Organization stuffed red ribbons in his hands and tied them around his bag at the bus stop, to remind him that he wasn't bleeding for his species. He failed his classes spectacularly that year, out of spite really. The truth was, maybe he didn't want something drilled in his spine. Maybe he didn't want to fight monsters to the death.

"If it weren't for my bad leg I'd be out there. Fighting! I got tested, in any case. You know my score? 75! I would have been a pilot!"

"Mine was 89," Anton said, and the man's face fell, then curled in anger.

"78," said the girl behind them.

"82," said the boy.

"96," Pamela said from her wheelchair, and she grinned at no one in particular. No one seemed to know what to say about that. Anton hadn't heard of a score that high. Now that was something.

Anton thought about that morning, after his own secret cry on the roof outside his bedroom window. That had always been his sanctuary, and it was impossible to imagine that he would never return to it. His grandmother was putzing around the house as he leaned over the radio in the sickly green, 70s era kitchen. She hadn't packed her mother's spoons, and Anton wondered if they should take them, maybe to sell.

"Reports are coming in that authorities have abandoned Chicago and San Francisco. Citizens should move immediately to their evacuation center. Take only what you can carry."

"We need to go, Grandma," he shouted and walked into her bedroom.

On her bed was an open suitcase and neat, folded rows. There was another row of glass eyed, real fur cats. His grandmother slowly tottered to the shelves, reached up, selected another cat, and set it carefully on the pastel quilt. She smoothed an errant tuft of hair on its head. Anton stomped to the bed and started shoving things in the bag. His grandmother gave a little cry of protest. Anton didn't stop. He kept shoving things in, ugly sweaters, long, cotton skirts, white tennis shoes. His grandmother tugged on his arm.

"It's okay, Anton. It's okay. I'll do it. I'll do it better."

But he packed the whole thing, and then shut it and carried it to the car. His grandmother followed him, holding a single kitten, with the wild tuft on his ear. She cradled it as they drove to their assigned evacuation area. Now he wished he'd taken the time and been gentle. He thought he'd have so much more time.

There was a final click and the elevator rose into the rain. The small group looked out into the rain at the airstrip that ran along the plateau. Anton could hear the waves crashing against the cliff, breaking the stone down one wave at a time. At the end of the runway, bobbing on its line like a toy, was a gondola. The impossibly thin, black chords flowed away from the cliffs, and disappeared into the gray, indistinct distance.

"You're kidding!" the boy said.

Diana tucked her tablet inside her jacket as she stepped into the storm. The wind and rain began undoing her careful bun. Anton hurried after her. Behind him he heard Pamela yell "Let go!" He glanced back as the boy recoiled from her chair, her fury turned toward him. She started rolling across the asphalt with purpose. The ground shook underneath them. After a few steps, it shook again.

"They're breaking through," Mr. Henderson yelled over the noise of the surf and the rain.

"No," Diana said, raising her voice and holding her hair out of her face. "That's ignition. The first ships are taking off."

Sure enough the ground shuddered again the mountain roared, as if it was erupting. Anton pressed his hands to his ears and turned to watch the launch. The ship rose from the side of the cliff, as if a piece of it had simply risen into the sky, followed by a long plume of flame and cloud of smoke. It rose into the sky, through the rain, swirling the clouds like a rock thrown into a pond. They ran on. At the edge of the cliff Mr. Henderson pulled open the door to the Gondola and practically shoved the rest of them inside. The man with the gun closed the door behind them.

"You will be able to see them if you look out the windows." Diana said, going back to her tablet.

Anton looked out the window as the car shuttered to life. Below them, hidden in the mist and gloom, massive creatures moved in the water. Three of them, no, four, five! They looked like ten-story-tall gorillas, massive and bulky, towering over the wreckage of the aircraft carriers they had already dismantled. Metal, meat, and fur were twisted together to form their bodies – like a bruise-colored, violent freight train. Jagged things, like black bone, jutted from their shoulders, elbows, and skulls. They moved through the mist and water like they belonged, creatures without predator, and only one, very small enemy. One of the things looked up and watched the tiny car, roughly the size of its paw. Its body tensed, like a cat watching a toy.

"Where did they come from?" Mr. Henderson whispered.

"You mean those specifically, or the Peers themselves?" Anton asked with some relish. Mr. Henderson glared at him and he shrugged. "We made them. They were invented by James Peerich, a solution to the loss of human life inherent in any combat and adopted by the army with enthusiasm. Simply boot up a Peer and aim it at a city. Normal problems with robotics – balance, perception, problem solving – were solved through a fusion of biological elements with technology. Problems of control were solved with shoving computers into the things' brains. That worked fine until they started reproducing. We're still not sure how they managed that."

Henderson looked pale and sat down. Anton looked down at the monsters as they bashed the cliff face with their arms, chewed with their mouths, even threw themselves against it. Why did they want to destroy us so badly?

He remembered standing with a bat in his grandmother's front yard over the crushed remains of her mailbox. Mrs. Anna Louise Christina Pauley, his dead mother's mother, held her hand out for the bat. He knew he should feel guilty for acting out, but instead he was angry. He felt that he was supposed to mourn his parents, to understand their loss and become better for it. But that heroic peace never came and he hated himself. He wanted to break his grandmother's head open. She took the bat away and dragged him into the house by the arm. I can't do this, Anton thought. He sat next to Diana with a sigh and pulled at his beard.

"My grandmother will be allowed to go?" Anton asked.

"They'll take everyone. Everyone is important now. Everyone is Earth," Diana said.

"Even the weak?" Anton asked.

"Yes. It was a possibility from the beginning. It was called Operation Grata. Theoretically we would reach a point where we no longer believed we could retake the earth. Contrition was designed to buy the human race one more year, or one more hour, or five more minutes."

Anton nodded. "You have a family, Mr. Henderson?"

"Yeah," Mr. Henderson said. "I—"

"Jesus Christ!" the boy yelled, his face pressed against the window. "It jumped."

Anton and Diana both leaped to their feet and ran to the window. Below them, the Peer that had been watching them crashed into the sea. The wave caused by its body rolled over the broken ships, sending them against the rocks again. It rose up on its feet again and roared, a noise like a freight train leaping off the tracks, screeching metal and thunder. The other monsters turned to look at it, like a litter of kittens watching their brother play. The thing leapt again, claws opening like semi-truck-sized scythes. The girl screamed. The lift rocked form the displaced air, but the Peer tumbled back to the water again.

"It's okay," Anton said, breathlessly. "It's okay."

The other monsters turned from the cliff face, moving

ponderously toward their comrade. They all looked up the tiny toy, their orange eyes reflecting the lights of the air strip, the moon, the stars, or something inside of them, burning away. They tensed to jump. Then they turned their heads, quickly, as if they all heard the same noise at once. Two more leviathans appeared around the corner of the cliffs. They were also mostly metal, shining in the dim light.

"There's our team," Anton said, excitedly pointing at them. He'd never actually seen one fighting before. He remembered seeing them once, from a great distance. They were walking toward Chicago, when the Peers first attacked. He climbed on the roof to watch them, squat metal humans the size of mountains, lumbering across the field beyond his little town. His grandmother yelled at him to come down, that instant, but he pretended he couldn't hear her. At the time, the creatures still represented hope: a chance to cleanse the world of human mistakes.

"Those are the piloted Peers. Second Gens," Anton went on. "The Peers were built to absorb impact from missiles and convert it into useful energy, like plants absorb sunlight and grow. It's very clever, until it's used against you, and it's probably how they managed to reproduce. We made them too adaptable. The Gen 2s have the same set up, but completely controlled with human pilots, physically strapped into the thing. They implant a tap into the pilots' spines. The circuits run through their –"

"Please stop!" the girl cried out.

She turned away from the window as the two groups met, their bodies swinging against each other. The Gen 2s were stronger, but slower, more awkward. Anton pressed his nose against the glass and watched a Peer dig his massive, building-sized teeth into the Gen 2s' arm. Then a wall of stone leapt up in front of him and he couldn't see. The gondola entered a cave, slowed, and stopped near a thin platform.

The door popped open and the group descended slowly, the weight of what they'd just seen was heavy on all of them. Anton couldn't tell if the low rumbling was the thunder, the monsters below, or the ships trying to get away. The thin platform ended in stairs, circling upward into the mountain. Anton looked down at Pamela.

"I'm sorry," Diana said. "It's the only way."

Anton lifted the girl onto his back. She didn't weight as much as he thought. They started up the stairs. Anton tried not to think about how much stone was above him, below him around him, waiting to fall if the Peers hit it hard enough. It would be all right if it happened fast enough, but if he was only partially crushed he might bleed for days before he died. He shuddered.

"You alright?" Pamela asked. "I'm not heavy, am I?"

"No. You're fine," Anton said.

There was another crash against the side of the cave. When he was younger he sat on the roof and watched the Gen 2s stomp off toward Chicago. They seemed like super heroes then, and he thought that, when he was old enough, he'd run away from his disapproving grandmother and become a pilot. He imagined himself as a hero of the world. When did he stop believing in that? Maybe it was when his neighbor's children stopped coming back – when they started losing. Though, honestly, it was probably when he found his grandmother crying because the neighbor called her grandson a coward.

"Don't go," she begged him, tears running down her face. "Don't let them convince you."

There were so many things he could say. He knew they were only looking for bodies to lay on top of their sons – to make a wall between themselves and danger, and maybe hide the faces of their beloved dead with strangers. They wanted to distance themselves from so many things. They wanted to save themselves, and he couldn't blame them. But he had long outgrown doing his grandmother harm for no reason.

"I promise," he said. "Now stop crying."

"What were you thinking about?" Pamela asked.

"Fake cats." "Oh yeah?"

"Yeah. My grandmother has all these fake cats that are made from real fur. She loves them though. I think they're real to her. I think she likes being so close to creating a little life."

"That's a stupid thing to think about at a time like this," Pamela said.

Anton started to shrug and then remembered he was carrying her. He was such a selfish prick and he knew that now, after all this. Pamela probably had earned her bitterness the honest way.

"Do you know where we're going?" he asked.

"Yes. I figured it out."

The cliff shook underneath them and the lights flickered. "How long with the electricity hold out?" Mr. Henderson asked.

"The generators will shut down automatically at 2:00 tomorrow. The world will mostly be dark by then," Diana answered.

They reached the top of the stairs and the group came to a halt. What they were looking at was surreal and it took them all a minute to process it. They were in a second bunker, exactly like the one they left. The brushed silver doors of ships stood at the end. Beside them, a line of Gen 2s hunched silently. The only difference was that the massive bunker was empty. No one waited for the shuttles. No pilots waited at the mechs.

"What is this?" Mr. Henderson said.

"Evacuation Bay 2," Diana said, striding past the group to a small control panel. She set the tablet into its place on the wall. "There weren't enough people to fill both. Diana Smith reporting at A113. I am preparing the team now." Then she turned to them. "We don't have time for implants. The connections will drill directly into your spine. It won't hurt. When you reach the battlefield, do not hold back. Whatever you can give us in the next twenty minutes is everything you have left to give."

"What?" the girl said.

"We're the team." Pamela said impatiently. "We're getting in those things and fighting. We're going to buy them time to escape. Another hour. Another five minutes."

"Hell no!" Mr. Hernandez yelled.

His voice echoed through the empty room and the teenagers flinched. Diane turned to him, fury showing just a little under her damp hair, her ruined makeup.

"We are safe for now, Mr. Hernandez, but they will break through. There are teams across the world, buying time," Diane said. "They will break through and kill your children! Go!"

Still he didn't move and she gave a tiny nod. The soldier stepped forward and struck him across the shoulder with the gun. The girl squeaked as the soldier pushed him forward. He stumbled toward the huge machines. The boy and girl stepped up beside Pamela and Anton.

"What do you think?" Anton said, because he was really curious.

"I'll help you," the boy said to Pamela. She shot him a look of fury. "Don't. There's no choice."

"Fine," she said.

They were going to die. They were all going to die. All past and future versions of them were going to die. The little boy on the roof, holding his action figures, may as well have been crushed to pulp under the monster's feet. No, Anton thought, then he wouldn't be here. He watched Pamela and the teenagers approach the machines.

"What happens if we survive this? What happens if we win?" he asked.

"I don't know," Diana said.

He nodded. "What about you?"

"I have to stay here. Someone has to monitor you," Diane said. "I'll stay here until the end. I won't leave."

"Thank you," Anton said and held out his hand. She looked at it for a long moment and shook it.

"It will hurt," she said, the only favor she could give him.

And it did, though the sound was worse as the cable drilled through his bone. He could feel his blood drip over his shoulder and wondered how he would clean that, before remembering it didn't matter. He screamed. Somewhere past that he heard voices crackle to life in his head, Mr. Henderson crying and someone, maybe Pamela, screaming in defiance, fierce and full of pain, in a place at the edge of joy and horror. His mech rocked forward and he fell into the ocean. He could feel, vaguely, the tide pulling at him, like snow on his boots. Then he stood and turned to see if he could spot the ships leave the atmosphere, to say good-bye and good luck.

MORY TAKES FLIGHT

Anna O'Brien

Anna is a writer and veterinarian currently living in central Maryland.

"Mory Takes Flight" first appeared in Unlocked: Short Stories from the Frederick Writers' Salon.

A crow told Amira she was pregnant. This was such an ominous sign, the young woman, in tears, sought the most respected oracle in Cyprus the next day.

Yes, a crow's triplicate caw at midnight on the eve of a harvest moon foretells a cursed mother, the old woman agreed, fingering the long string of black beads around her withered neck. She bobbed her head like a chicken and thrust a gnarled dark hand onto Amira's belly. "But I think maybe the baby bears the curse, not you," the old woman said, closing her milky wet eyes and rubbing Amira's stomach with such gentleness unique to a soothsayer that Amira became unnerved.

"A mother wears the curse of her child," Amira replied, pulling away from the old woman's hand. Amira tightened her shawl around her narrow shoulders and pulled back the long black hair that trailed her face like jungle vines. "What should I do?"

"Does your husband suspect anything?"

Amira was silent. There was no husband, only a boy, naïve like herself. Sweet and earnest. Young and tender.

Amira shook her head and looked at the dirt floor. The old woman grunted and turned toward the shelf behind her. Reedy fingers danced in midair as she considered the dusty glass bottles on the shelf—some full, others nearly empty.

She handed a stout brown bottle with a cracked cork and yellow label to Amira.

"Take this," she said. "Drink about half tonight and the rest in two days if nothing happens."

Amira took the bottle tentatively. "What is supposed to happen?"

The old woman squinted at Amira then tapped Amira's belly with a crooked index finger, as if testing a melon for ripeness. Somewhere outside a rooster crowed and the hut was becoming stuffy as the morning sun rose higher in the sky, its golden beams spying on them through joints in the sheet metal walls.

"It will take care of your problem, my dear. Now, if you please," she turned a palm upwards, seeking payment.

Amira burst into tears, dropping the bottle on the floor. Brown glass shattered and thick, dark fluid oozed toward a low spot.

The old woman looked not unkindly at Amira. A familiar scenario, these raw girls, almost feral. "Then I'm afraid you really only have one option," she whispered.

Amira wiped the tears from her cheeks with a shaky hand and leaned forward for the answer.

"Run!" the old woman hissed.

Amira bolted from the hut. She was never seen in her childhood village again.

|

A small, thin boy crawls under a giant, tightly woven net strung from the top of an ancient olive tree. When he gets to the junction of the net to the ground, he finds three trapped birds: two golden orioles and one bunting. Grabbing the two orioles in one fist and the bunting in the other, he quickly checks the net for holes. Finding none, he maneuvers out.

Sitting in the shade of the tree, the boy considers his catch. The two orioles are stunned, breathing heavily through gaping pointed orange beaks but the bunting, a local species, remains quiet, contemplating the boy as calmly as the boy contemplates the small, brown bird.

The boy knows one of his Uncle Joseph's rules: don't hunt the local birds. He tosses the bunting gently into the air. It catches flight and retreats to an upper branch of the olive tree, giving a rough and throaty caw before it flies away, the branch bouncing in its wake.

The boy looks at the remaining two orioles, knowing they'd provide a much more musical song if he were to set them free. But it's meat over music, as his uncle says. The boy never gets any of the meat.

||

Amira doesn't approve of her brother Joseph's side business or her son's involvement, but she keeps quiet. Her brother was valiant enough, at least in his own mind, to provide refuge seven years ago to his pregnant unwed sister and they both, as self-imposed exiles, try to find comfort in each other. They've formed a somewhat functional family unit as long as everyone contributes.

Joseph unloads barges on the river but it's unpredictable work, equally dependent on the fickleness of local politics and the capricious nature of the river. As supplement, Joseph hunts the migratory birds that fly over Cyprus on their way to northern Africa. He peddles their delicate meat as a street vendor. Amira washes clothes.

Mory, Amira's son, has recently started helping Joseph with bird hunting. Mory is adept at the work; his small size makes it easy for him to check the nets and his agile fingers can easily set ground snares and pluck the tiny birds from sticky traps in the trees. This is solitary, quiet work given its questionable legality. This, too, fits Mory, given his harelip and his general avoidance of the villagers' stares.

On his way home, Mory checks another net and five snares he set the day before. All are empty so he continues through the marginal forest of olive and date trees, breathing in the humid air tinged with the sea, his steps light. The orioles in his hand remain still until one of them speaks.

"Goodness, boy, what on earth are you doing?" a crisp male voice calls out.

Mory freezes. Rarely does he encounter anyone else in the woods as he checks his uncle's traps. Even the other children in the village won't follow Mory into the woods. It's a respite from their taunts. Mory crouches next to a stately date tree and looks around.

"Hey, hey boy," the voice says. "Right here. Say, what's the date?"

Mory looks at the two orioles in his hand. One remains listless, half-dead. The other is looking directly at Mory, its head cocked slightly to the side.

"It's Tuesday," Mory whispers shyly.

"But the date? The date?" The voice is insistent.

Mory shrugs. "I don't know."

"You don't know what day it is? At Piccadilly, all the paperboys know the date."

Having established he's not being followed, Mory continues his trek home, holding the conversational oriole in front of him, a specimen to be examined far more closely than any previous bird.

"What's a Piccadilly?" Mory asks the bird.

"Not what but where, boy," says the bird. "Piccadilly—it's in London. Bright lights, cabbies, newspapers on the corner."

"Is that near Rome?" he asks.

"Rome!" the bird laughs, jumping a little in Mory's fist. "What's wrong with you, boy? Haven't heard of England, have you? I must be further from home than I thought. Say, is this Italy, then?"

"Cyprus," says Mory, the word exaggerating his lisp. He ponders the bird's geography lesson. "You flew all the way from England?" He looks closer at the small bird, incredulous that such a tiny creature, so light and scrawny in his hand, could make its way such a great distance.

The bird puffs his chest. "Yes, I suppose I did. Not quite sure how, really, but I am hungry. Say," says the bird, suddenly suspicious. "What exactly have you got planned?" The bird peers over at his doppelganger, which is now dead.

It is obvious to Mory that he can't hand this talking bird over to his uncle. Nor can he walk into the village and introduce everyone to his new friend. Mory has seen enough so far in his short life to realize not everyone thinks unique things are special.

Returning home empty-handed is also risky. The last time he returned without birds, his uncle hit Mory with a belt, saying he hadn't laid enough snares, he wasn't mending his nets, and if he showed up without any birds again, his backside would resemble his cleaved face.

Mory considers the dead oriole. It will have to do. Freshly dead was tolerable—bloat hadn't set in yet and the meat was still fresh.

"I have no plans," Mory says to the bird. "Nice meeting you, sir." Mory tosses the yellow bird gently into the air like he did the bunting and watches as the bright speck climbs higher into the hazy sky, its melodious call becoming lost in the wind.

III

Walking into the village, Mory wonders if the excitement of his conversation is obvious. A few villagers look at him a little closer than usual. Instead of turning away, others bear him a glance. Is he smiling? Mory has learned never to smile in public, as it exaggerates his lip defect. Did they hear him laugh? He tries to act as solemn and shy as he normally does, and heads straight to Joseph's house.

Entering the empty cottage, Mory makes his way to the back to his uncle's workroom. Old rusty snares, mangled ropes, and patchwork segments of old netting hang from hooks along the wall. Just before reaching the back wall where the holding cages for the day's catch are located, Mory passes a tall, ovoid cage with polished bars. His uncle's latest investment is a falcon, trained by Sicilians to catch small migratory birds. Assured that the raptor would pay for itself quickly, Joseph has developed a volatile relationship with the cunning and beautiful bird, haughty and unpredictably ambivalent toward its predatory role.

Joseph curses the falcon mercilessly when it returns from an unfruitful hunt, turning red in the face when he can't remember the Italian hunting commands. When the bird does return with a swallow or a shrike in its talons, Joseph dances like a little boy, slathering the falcon with praise and small pieces of dried goat meat.

The falcon appears impervious to Joseph's moods, only grasping the man's leathered arm with its scaly yellow talons, not a shred of emotion visible in its black unblinking eyes. With Amira, however, it exudes warmth, gently taking pieces of potato or fish from her hand. Mory remains wary of the raptor, which is as tall as his own torso. He is unnerved by the bird's stare, which seems to follow only him.

When not hunting, the falcon stays locked in the oval cage,

the small bronze key in the top drawer of Joseph's nightstand. Joseph puts a dingy sheet over the cage at night.

When Mory passes the falcon in its cage, he hears another voice.

"Dead birds won't do," it hisses. "He only likes live ones."

Mory is sure he is alone in the house, with his mother still washing clothes at the village well and his uncle at the river until dinner. Mory stops and stares at the falcon.

"I always bring back live birds," the voice brags. "He'll be mad at you."

This voice is quite unlike the oriole's. Where the yellow bird's dripped with cautious congeniality, this raspy voice hits like pinpricks. Mory flinches.

"He, he doesn't mind them when they're just dead," Mory stutters, realizing that his earlier conversation with the oriole was not a fluke.

"Just dead?" the falcon sneers. "What's just dead? Dead is dead. Like you'll be when he gets home."

The little boy's heart hammers in his thin chest. "What do you know? You're just a bird."

"Just a bird?" the falcon scoffs, producing a laugh that sounds as if it has passed through miles of clogged pipes. "If you can hear me, does that make you just a boy?"

Mory doesn't know what to make of any of it. Confused and scared, he grabs the dirty sheet and flings it over the falcon's cage. Then he runs to the back of the room, tossing the dead oriole into the holding cage and tears out of the house. Mory hears the falcon laughing as he passes through the doorway.

IV

Not all of them speak. Some are dead or die en route to the village, their little hearts unable to bear the stress.

Others—most others—remain simply as captive birds should: jumpy, erratic, and tense.

Over the next few weeks, Mory talks to dozens of birds. A whitethroat caught in a sticky trap came from the beaches of Normandy; a red-breasted robin in a snare reported from Finland; a jay caught in a net only repeated one phrase: "Those men, always bugging me."

Mory begins to introduce himself to every victim of his traps, wanting to establish his role as confidant and then rescuer, as he releases the birds that speak. He brings back the silent birds for his uncle.

Mory also notices that he is the only one who can hear the birds. The first time the falcon accosted Mory with Joseph in the house, Mory jumped from fright so badly he fell on his face onto the dirt floor, knocking an old, rotting net on top of himself. Joseph looked over at him but didn't say a word. The falcon cackled maniacally.

What Mory begins to notice about birds, however, Amira is noticing about Mory. One night, while helping his mother clean dishes after supper, Amira grabs Mory's face and looks at him intensely.

"Are you feeling all right?" Amira asks.

"Yes," says Mory, squirming under her grasp.

"I think your eyes are changing color," she says, her brow furrowing. "They used to be a beautiful brown, like an oak. Now," she squints, "they look almost black."

Mory wiggles out of her hands and looks down at the ground, sensitive to others' comments about his appearance.

"And you're acting strangely," she continues. "I've watched you in the back. The other day, you were just staring at the sky."

Mory has taken the habit of watching birds in flight,

wondering who is talking, where they are going, where they came from. He blushes.

"You like the birds, don't you?" Amira asks. She puts her hands on Mory's bony shoulders. Her hands are cracked and she smells of soap and lye.

Mory nods.

Amira sighs. "So do I, baba, so do I. But, Joseph says once he pays off the falcon, we can start saving to get your lip fixed." She pulls Mory toward her, hugging him. "There are doctors that can come and do the surgery here," she whispers into his dark hair. "Agar, at the well, says they do a good job. She says they fixed her niece perfectly, not even a scar."

Mory hugs Amira back then pulls away and gives her a small smile. He is dying to tell someone about the talking birds. If he could tell anyone about this discovery, it would be his mother, his only ally.

"Momma," he begins, and then hesitates. She is already worried, why bring up something else?

"Yes, baba?" she says.

"Mmmm, where is Normandy?"

Amira gives a surprised little laugh. "Normandy? What an odd thing to ask. Where did you hear about Normandy?"

Mory shrugs, his face burning.

"Normandy is in France," Amira says. "Where they talk funny and eat snails. Ooh la la!" She reaches out to pinch Mory, who runs away shrieking with laughter.

V

Mory never accompanies his uncle when he hunts with the falcon.

"Man's work," boasted Joseph the first time he took the falcon out. "Not fit for women or children." Usually after a successful hunt, Joseph goes directly to the street to sell his delicacies. Grilled on an open pit, the dark, bite-sized meat is sometimes sprinkled with sugar, sometimes pepper and salt.

One day, however, Joseph returns with live catches, saying he doesn't feel well enough to sell on the street that night. He places his bounty in the holding cage, feeds the raptor its meal of goat meat, and covers its cage with the sheet. Then Joseph goes to bed.

After supper, Mory is helping his mother again with the dishes when he hears a shout: "Amira! Is that you?"

Mory freezes, all color draining from his small oval face.

"Amira! Amira! Praise be! It is you!"

Amira hands Mory a dish to dry and when he doesn't take it, she looks over at him and gasps.

"Mory! What's wrong?"

With the voice in the background still frantically calling his mother's name, Mory begins to cry. How could his mother not hear the voice?

"What's wrong, baba?" Amira pleads, embracing Mory in her arms, holding his head to her damp apron.

"The bird," says Mory into the faded cloth that smells of spices and vinegar. "Can't you hear it?"

"What, baba? What bird?" asks Amira.

Mory cries harder. "It's calling your name, Momma, the bird. It's calling your name."

Amira holds Mory out at arm's length. "What are you talking about? That thing?" She points to the covered falcon cage.

Mory shakes his head and leads Amira to the back of the room where the captive songbirds are held. There are several in the cage but only one is at the front, peering out. It is a plover, native to Cyprus. Joseph is letting the falcon hunt local birds.

The plover begins jumping around erratically when Amira approaches the cage.

"My god, there you are! Amira! After all these years! Boy, let me out. Let me out to see my daughter."

Mory reaches into the cage and pulls out the little brown bird, its white belly bright in the darkness. Gently, he holds it in his palm for his mother to see.

"It says it's your mother," he says.

Amira's soft face hardens. "Mory," she says. "That is a cruel thing to say. Why would you make something like that up?"

Shocked at her disbelief, Mory cries, "It's true! It talked to me! I can hear birds talk!"

A flame burns behind Amira's dark eyes. "I will not have these stories in my house!" she growls, not loud enough to disturb Joseph only a closed door away. "You put that bird back and return to the kitchen right now."

Sobbing, Mory pleads, "Momma! It's true! It called your name!"

Amira reaches back and slaps Mory in the face. He recoils in shock and hurt; his mother has never struck him before.

"There will be no witchcraft animal talking in this house, do you understand me?" Amira says in a voice so low Mory can hardly hear her. The finger she shakes in front of his dripping nose trembles and she is on the verge of tears herself.

"How dare you strike that poor boy," the bird scolds. "Amira! I shall prove it. Boy, tell her my name: Savina Maria Ionnou. Growing up, she had a small white dog named Georgi and when she was ten, she tried to make bread by herself and almost burned the house down."

Mory relays this information to Amira who slowly shakes her

head in disbelief, holding a hand over her mouth. The little bird peers at Amira. Everyone is motionless.

"How can this be?" Amira asks. "The other day at the well, Agar said she heard my mother was sick. I worried she would die. I haven't seen her in so many years." Rivulets of tears trace lines down Amira's cheeks.

"There, there," says the bird. "Yes, pneumonia, they said. Fluid in the lungs. Next thing, I'm flying, then hit. Something big. Dark, stuffed in a sack. Now this! Amira, what are you doing here?"

Mory acts as translator while Amira and his grandmother, whom he has never met, catch up, although Amira leaves several vital pieces of information out. She doesn't mention Mory is her son, or that she is living with Joseph, her older brother who ran away from gambling debts as a young man.

Soon, the bird appears to grow weak. Alarmed, Amira grabs Mory's arm. "What's happening? What should we do?"

Mory understands the toll that the stress of capture takes on these animals. "We have to let her go," he says. He motions toward Joseph's bedroom door. "Otherwise she'll die."

Amira nods. "Is this why you like birds so much?" she asks. "Because you can talk to them?"

"They don't all talk," whispers Mory. "But the ones that do, I let go."

"Of course," Amira says, giving explicit understanding to her son. "Of course." As they walk outside with the bird, Amira hesitates. "What about the others?"

"Uncle will know," Mory says. "He'll know we let them out. He'll be angry."

"Mory, that one little bird has the soul of my mother. What other secrets do those creatures carry?"

"Please don't let them out," Mory begs, thinking of the belt.

Amira shoos him away. "I'll take care of it, don't worry, baba."

She meets Mory at the back of the yard with her arms full of birds of all colors. "Goodbye, Momma," she calls to the plover and on the count of three, mother and son toss the birds into the air. A rainbow takes flight, yellows brighter, reds more murderous, green more verdant in the muted light of dusk. Amira has never seen anything more beautiful.

They walk back into the house together. Amira is deep in thought. She pauses by the falcon's cage. "Mory," she says, fingering the hem of the sheet that covers the cage. "What about the falcon? Does it say anything?" She looks almost dreamy.

Mory debates. Maybe he'll tell her about the unpleasant falcon later. He shakes his head. Although worried about Joseph's reaction, tonight, he feels relief. Someone finally knows his secret.

When Mory passes by the falcon's covered cage on his way to bed, he hears a familiar gargling laugh. "I get to do what I want and I'm in a cage," the falcon says. "You and your lovely mother will get punished for your reckless freedom."

That night, Mory dreams he is caught in one of his own nets. Flailing against the rope, he watches as his uncle appears. With yellow talons, Joseph reaches into the net and pulls Mory out. Then Joseph eats him.

VI

Amira is able to diffuse Joseph's reaction to the lost birds because that's what she calls them. She pleads ignorance and says Joseph must not have shut the door properly because she and Mory found the cage wide open the next morning, empty. Joseph scoffs but says nothing.

Between Mory and Amira it is mutually understood that

Joseph is not to find out about Mory's gift. Amira begins to firmly believe Mory is talking to the souls of dead people and asks Mory to milk the birds for information, like names, occupation, what they last remember. Mory complies but often these interrogations do not work. The birds are more interested in asking Mory where they are and what day it is. Mory is too shy to pry and ignorant of most dates as he can't read and time passes without his care. He is instead content with a geography lesson.

The birds tell Mory about Brussels, the Eiffel Tower, the Isle of Man, and the tulip fields of Rotterdam. Amira brings home a worn map of Europe one afternoon and points out West Germany, Portugal, and their very own island in the Mediterranean. Mother and son spend the rest of the evening imagining what these places must look like.

It is during this evening, sprawled on the floor of their shared bedroom, giggling about the boot shape of Italy, the faded colors of the map flickering in the light of the oil lamp, that Amira thinks back to her own experience with the raven years ago. If this was the curse foretold, and not the harelip, then she was accepting of it. In fact, it hardly seemed like a curse at all. She starts to feel a weight lift off her chest. The anticipation of a fate far worse than this is dissipating. She feels almost free.

Almost.

A few days later, while making Mory's bed, Amira notices a few small, white, downy feathers among the sheets. Thinking her son simply isn't washing up properly before bed, she chastises him and then forgets about the incident. A few more days pass and she finds more downy feathers along with two larger ones, bright yellow with a black border.

"Mory," she calls, but the boy is out checking traps. Puzzled, she begins to pull out Mory's clothes. Inside his threadbare shirts are more white feathers and in the seat of his pants, more yellow ones.

An odd feeling begins to overwhelm Amira as she contemplates the changes she is seeing in her son. Just then, Joseph appears in the doorway of the bedroom, proudly holding a sack full of panicked birds. "We'll make some money tonight!" he says and continues to the back of the house.

The odd feeling in Amira's chest flutters into horror and knocks her onto the bed.

VII

During his daily checks of the snares, nets, and sticky traps, Mory lets increasing numbers of birds go, regardless of whether they can speak. Releasing those caught in sticky traps requires him to wet the birds' wingtips and feet with his own saliva in order to clean off the adhesive goo. The bitter taste of the glue leaves him nauseous, so he stops setting sticky traps altogether.

Joseph begins to notice the drastic reduction in birds. Work on the barges has lately kept Joseph from regularly hunting with the falcon, so the side business ceases to be profitable.

At first, Joseph teases Mory about it, especially if Amira is around. But after several days of Mory returning with only one or two dead or nearly dead jays, Joseph grabs Mory by the shirt collar when Amira is out at the well.

"If I can't pay for this falcon, you'll never get your face fixed," he snarls so close to Mory that the boy is showered in spittle. Joseph gives Mory a shake, then walks out.

Mory then hears the falcon laugh. "Poor little yellow bird," it says. "Watch out behind you."

Mory looks over to where he and Joseph were just standing. Three yellow feathers with a black border lie on the ground.

Mory rushes over and scoops them up while the falcon giggles like a madman.

VIII

Amira soon notices Mory is losing weight. "You're not eating enough," she clucks at him, pouring half of her own fish stew into his bowl at dinner. "Look at how skinny he is," she says to Joseph. "Don't you think he's too thin?"

Joseph barely looks up from his own bowl, distracted. "Maybe if he caught more birds, we'd have more to eat," he replies.

Later that night, while they are getting ready for bed, Amira steals a glance at her son as he dresses into his nightgown. Convinced he looks different, Amira turns toward Mory in their bedroom.

"Let me see you," she says softly.

Embarrassed, Mory stands in front of his mother in nothing but his underwear.

"You're shrinking," Amira says. "The hems on your pants? Lately, always dirty because they are dragging the ground. And your shoulders," she grabs his bare shoulders in both hands, feeling his slight, boney frame through warm skin. "So very narrow. And your legs." She kneels down to the floor to examine stilt-like appendages with hardly any meat. His bare dirty feet are scaly.

"Mory." She takes her son's hand. The skin between his fingers feels prickly. A small white feather is lodged between his index and middle finger. She plucks it out. Mory winces as a drop of blood grows in the webbing. "What's happening to you?"

Mory begins to cry. He's been wondering the same thing since the very first oriole spoke. When he first noticed feathers in his clothes, in his bed, floating in the latrine, he didn't feel any different. Now, his heartbeat is always a rapid staccato. He is nervous, agitated.

"It's all right, baba," Amira says, hugging him. "I think I know. Embrace your gift. It was meant to be, from before you were born."

That night, Mory lies awake listening to the songs of the birds outside his window. His skin is sore where feathers are erupting with the heat of a blister. Will I be able to fly, he wonders. He watches the top of the giant olive tree sway in the breeze, illuminated by moonlight. He flexes his puny arms, imagining what it would be like to lift his own body off the ground and climb through the sky, visiting places like Copenhagen and Lisbon. If he could fly, then yes, it would be all right.

IX

The next day, Mory walks tenderly out to the woods to check his nets and snares. His feet feel pinched and the blisters between his fingers now extend up his arms. He is feverish.

When he arrives at the first net, he immediately notices something is very wrong. Large holes pock the net and in certain places it is torn completely, hanging impotently from dangling branches.

There is no way Mory can repair the damage. He carefully removes what is left of the delicate but strong woven rope and places it in his bag as salvage to be cannibalized by other nets for repair.

Moving to the next net not more than a quarter mile away, Mory finds remnants of another destroyed trap. With shaking hands, he again removes the remains.

Stomach sick with the fear of how Joseph will react to two destroyed nets, Mory hurries down his usual path in the woods and almost runs directly into his mother.

"Mory!" Amira exclaims. She laughs after her initial shock.

There is a wild and exhilarated look in her eyes that Mory has never seen before.

"Mory, look what I've done!" She pulls out a pair of kitchen shears from her laundry bag as well as three of Mory's own snares, disabled and smashed.

Mory gasps, incredulous at the very idea that his own mother would sabotage his uncle's work. "Momma! My snares! Did you? The nets?"

"Yes, baba!" she says, her voice breathy and light, a school-girl's rapturous glee. "You won't have to trap birds anymore!"

Mory's joy and love for his mother almost bursts his flut-tering heart but the ecstasy is tempered by the thought of his uncle's most certainly violent rebuttal. "But what about Uncle? He'll whip both of us," Mory says.

"He will not," Amira declares. "We will tell him thieves ran through the forest, stole all his birds, and destroyed his nets and snares. I'll have Agar spread the story at the well."

Mory nods but wonders if Joseph would believe rumors propagated by an old woman at the village well.

"And look," Amira whispers, almost to herself. She touches Mory's face. "Soon you'll have a beak. And you won't need surgery after all."

Mory reaches up and touches his nose, which feels hard and very pointed. He hasn't been down to the creek in days and without seeing his reflection, he has been unable to appreciate the rapid changes in his appearance.

Amira grabs Mory by the hand. "Come and show me where the rest of your snares are," she says. "We must get rid of them all. We are setting them all free."

X

Amira and Mory return by mid-morning, having destroyed

all the nets and disabled all snares. Any birds caught the night before are released. Mory can barely walk by the time they return.

"Lie down," Amira says to Mory when they reach the house. "I'll make you some tea."

As Mory lies on his back waiting for his mother's return, he feels he is on the verge of popping. His arms are now covered in feathers and his breath makes a whistling noise as he exhales through small, rigid nostrils. He is losing his fingers as they meld into one feathered stalk. His belly is expanding as his chest shrinks and his torso folds forward.

He drags a feathered appendage over his upper lip, feeling for the congenital split. It is almost completely gone and in its place a fusion between lip and nose, hard and pointed. Then his eyes catch a glimpse of the beautiful yellow feathers with black trim that are sprouting from his shoulders.

Mory begins to lose track of time when Amira doesn't appear with his tea. He has only his fluttering heart for a metronome. Afraid she's encountered Joseph, Mory means to leap out of bed to look for her when he finds he has shrunk so much he would have tumbled out and not been able to open the door.

Finally, Amira enters the room. She looks triumphantly radiant but her visage turns bittersweet as she looks at Mory's bed only to see a small, yellow bird. Tears well up in her eyes but she smiles. She steps over to the bed and picks Mory up, cradling him in her palm. Until this moment, Mory hasn't grasped the extent of just how small he's become and he peeps in surprise. His heartbeat finally fits his body.

Amira laughs. "Little Mory!" she coos as she holds the bird to her breast. "Look how beautiful you've become!" She clutches him close as she walks out of the house to the back where the large olive tree stands. "I suppose you must now learn to fly."

Amira is holding him so close and he is so excited that it isn't until she places him carefully on the dusty ground that he notices a key dangling from a chain around her neck. It is the key to the falcon's cage.

Mory's tiny feet buckle underneath him at the sight of the key. He begins chirping madly.

Amira giggles and squats over Mory, the key swinging back and forth between her breasts. "I don't know how mama birds do it," she says. "Just flap your wings as hard as you can."

Mory doesn't care now about flying. He has to know why his mother has the falcon's key. He continues to chirp and screech.

"What a noisy little thing you've become," his mother playfully chides. "Now go, baba, go be with all the other souls that we've set free."

She scoops Mory back into her hands. "I think maybe you need a little boost." She gives a dainty kiss to the side of Mory's body and with a gentle yet firm toss, Mory finds himself suddenly in the air.

Falling, Mory unfolds his still achy wings. He swoops and swerves and heaves until he feels a firm pillow of air beneath his fully extended wings. Then, with one mighty downward push, he goes up, then up, then up.

He hears Amira below him squeal with delight, calling his name. He chirps in response, preoccupied with the exhaustive yet somehow restorative feeling of the beating of his own wings.

Amira remains near the olive tree, hands shading her eyes from the early afternoon sunlight. She watches as her son rises in the sky, becoming just a bright yellow speck surrounded by blue. She is terrified yet sublimely happy.

Then, out of the corner of her eye, Amira sees a large, dark object swoop down from the sky. When she squints, she can make out a creamy throat and yellow talons, the very talons she released in her enthusiasm for freedom just a few hours before.

She watches, horrified, as the falcon gains on Mory, whose movements are still erratic. The falcon circles then dives, executing a silent blow that knocks Mory into a tumble.

Mory's wind is knocked out of him and he feels dizzy. The falcon grabs Mory by a wing and carries him upward, dangling. The talons dig into Mory's tender skin. He bleeds. A strange, hollow feeling grows in Mory as he realizes he is unable to cry.

As the pair rises in the sky, Mory gets a view of his island below. He sees the river and can make out a barge. The blue sea in the distance cuts a hazy horizon. He can no longer hear Amira screaming.

The falcon feigns dropping Mory then crushes him with both talons. Mory feels a bone pop.

"The date? What's the date, yellow bird?" the falcon cackles.

The falcon works himself into a laughing rage as the pair flies out to sea. Mory's sight grows fuzzy. He is exhausted.

"April 13," he whispers. Although it is June, his mother's birthday and Christmas are the only dates he knows.

"Eh?" The falcon slows to quiet the wind. It stops laughing.

"April 13," Mory repeats.

"Liar!" the falcon shrieks.

The pair encounters a draft of warm air and soars on a pillow of upward pressure. Then, more to itself than to Mory, "Doesn't feel like April."

"Take me back," Mory whimpers. "Take me back to Momma."

The falcon gives a harsh, gargled laugh. "I take orders from no one, especially little lying yellow birds."

It releases Mory and swoops west, toward Sicily.

Mory falls, his heart quiet.

Amira still stands under the olive tree, weeping. Mory is gone. The falcon is gone. The forest behind her is silent except for one harsh caw. A crow sits above her on a dying branch. It picks at a shriveled green olive, and then lets the pit fall to the ground. It looks at Amira as it clatters its beak.

Amira picks up the biggest stone she can find. She throws it at the crow and howls.

CALL CENTER BLUES

Carrie Cuinn

Carrie Cuinn is an author, editor, college student, and geek. In her spare time she works toward a degree in Creative Writing, listens to music, watches indie films, cooks everything, reads voraciously, and sometimes gets enough sleep. Find her online at @CarrieCuinn or at http://carriecuinn.com.

Previously published at Daily Science Fiction, November 2011

"Thank you for calling F.A.X. Unlimited. My name is Claire. How can I help you?"

"My household unit isn't working," a man's voice said gruffly. "I keep giving it commands, but they don't work."

"Ok sir, I'm happy to help you with that. Can I get your account number?" He rattled off a string of numbers, which I entered into my terminal. Out of the corner of my eye, I could see Patty taking another call, her head moving slowly in time with her dialogue. As long as she was still on that call, she wouldn't be able to take the next one. No such luxury for me, as I was currently IMing an encryption key to a factory manager in Bangalore, and simultaneously replying to an email about the new style and color options for the upcoming year. Meanwhile, my client's account opened up in front of me. "Thank you for your patience Mr. Holden. I just need to verify a little information before we can proceed. Are you still living at Apartment 24C, Burr Building, City Level 12?"

"Yes," he sighed. "Nothing's changed, your machine just doesn't work."

"I am sorry to hear that, sir, and we are going to get her fixed for you. Now, you have a May model, delivered to you 78 days ago. She's still under warranty so there will be no charge for this service call." I cringed as I said that. Knowing they didn't have to pay by the minute made some clients extra chatty, and I still had to troubleshoot that software download for a couple of dozen heavy labor models in India. "What kind of issues are you having with her?"

"She doesn't do anything."

"The unit doesn't turn on?"

"No, she's on. She's sitting on the sofa right now, staring at me."

"Have you tried turning her off and on again?"

"Yeah, I've done that. Doesn't help. She looks all bright and happy, then she sees me, stops smiling, and sits down on the couch."

I scanned the contents of John Holden's file, looking for attachments or upgrades that might be conflicting with the base programming. "Can I ask what kinds of tasks you're asking her to perform?"

"Nothing weird!" he insisted, though of course they all did. "Normal stuff. Cooking, cleaning. This morning I told her to make bacon, and she crossed her arms."

Scanning his original order, I spotted it. "Sir, were you aware that you ordered the optional Care and Compassion package?"

"That's the niceness thing, right? Guy said it would make her sweet. I want sweet. But refusing to cook my bacon is not sweet!" he yelled, head turned away from the receiver. He wasn't yelling at me.

"Sir, please calm down. I'm certain we can get this taken care of." Patty waved at me, and I looked down to see another line blinking. I shook my head, and the older woman nodded in response. She pushed a few buttons, and the light disappeared from my phone, leaving me with just Mr. Crankypants to deal with for a moment. "Now Mr. Holden, I'm not sure if you were aware of this but that module makes your unit more receptive to your needs, but it also makes her more sensitive to any anger or negativity on your part. When you phrase your requests, are you putting them in the form of a question? Are you saying please?"

"What? Why would I have to ask? She's a damn robot!"

I sighed as quietly as possible. The client was in his early 80s, and clearly prejudiced. "Sir, I understand your frustration and of course the May unit is designed to fulfill all of your culinary and cleaning needs. She wants to help you, sir. It's in her programming. It's just that over time, the unit can balk at orders. She needs a bit of a gentle touch, is all."

"Too much work," he grumbled. "Can't I reboot her, start from scratch?"

"Yes, sir, of course you can, but doing so will only solve the problem temporarily. As she develops her personality and adapts to your needs, you may run into this problem again."

"Don't care. Easier than not getting my breakfast!" I forced a smile back onto my face (Always Answer With A Smile! our training taught us), advised Holden to turn his unit off, and sent the reboot order wirelessly. Soon enough the May unit was back to her original, helpful, bacon-cooking self.

Checking the clock, I logged the call and switched my terminal off. India would have to wait until tomorrow.

"Bad call?" Patty asked.

"Another jerk who doesn't care that his robot has, you know, actual feelings." Patty nodded in reply, and rolling my eyes, I grabbed a screwdriver from my desk drawer. Walking over to my coworker, I said, "Patty, could I please fix that loose lever? Your head-bobbing is driving me nuts."

"Oh, yes please," Patty replied happily, her wrinkled face joyful. "I was starting to get dizzy."

"I understand," I said, gently opening the other woman's neck to reveal a spring-and-lever system slightly out of whack. "It happens to me all the time."

THANK YOU

Many thanks to our patrons
and supporters, especially:

KE Jaeck

Tory Hoke

GriffinFire

Want to see your name here? Become a patron!
patreon.com/lunastation

 patreon

ABOUT THE COVER ARTIST

Sara Kipin is currently a senior illustration major attending the Maryland Institute College of Art in Baltimore. As a child, she was gifted many illustrated fantasy books from her family and has now taken that inspiration with her into her adult years. Once graduated, she hopes to use these aesthetics as a book illustrator or a preproduction artist.

Learn more about Sara and see her work at:

http://sarakipin.tumblr.com

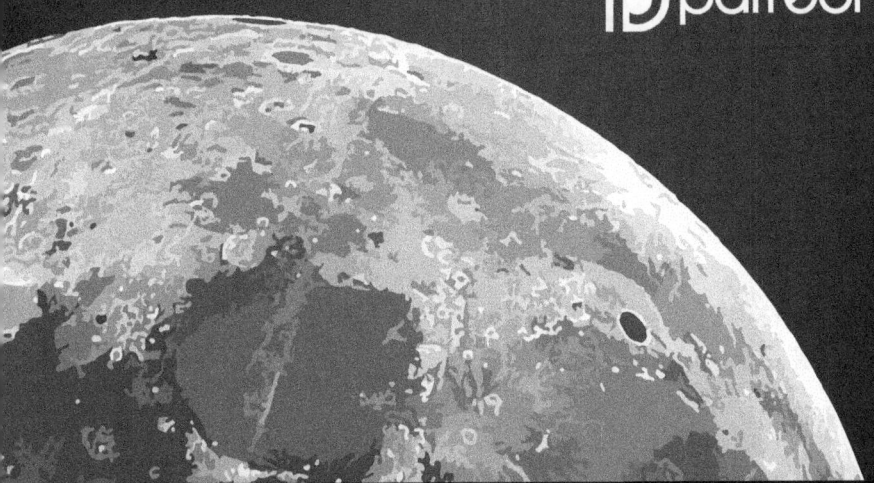